THE TEMPLAR
AND THE TEMPLE OF KÁROS

THE TEMPLAR
AND THE TEMPLE OF KÁROS
Part Two in the Series

Nigel Clayton

First published in Australia by Meni Publishing and Binding in
2006

Printed by CreateSpace, an Amazon.com Company.

Nigel Clayton
The Templar: And the Temple of Káros, Second Edition.
Part two in the Series
ISBN 978-0-9802985-5-0

1. Templars - Fiction. 2. Islam - Relations - Christianity History -
Fiction. 3. Istanbul (Turkey) - History - Siege, 1453 - Fiction. 4.
Turkey - History - Mehmed II,
1451-1481 - Fiction. 5. Byzantine Empire - Civilization -Fiction.
I. Title.

A823.4

IMPORTANT NOTE:

Mahon is the name denoting a boat employed by Mehmet's naval forces; the same vessel is referred to as a galleass by those of Constantinople.

Many seafaring vessels within this book are referred to as boat, as opposed to ship, due to my interpretation of the description given in the dictionary.

OTHER TITLES BY THIS AUTHOR

The Long Road to Rwanda
Colonies of Earth
Fall of the Inca Empire
Inca Myths and Way of Life
The Templar: and the City of God [Part 1 in the series]
The Templar: and the Cross of Christ [Part 3]
Amazon [Part 4 of the Templar series]
Underworld
Spacescape
Space Opera – Heaven and Hell
Tom of Twofold Bay
The Zuytdorp Survivors
Afghan
Afghan: The Script
Chivalry
The Caves of Hiroshima
Scourge
The Cure
Furious George
This Pestilence, Bergen-Belsen
Templar, Assassination, Trial & Torture
Underworld
Dreamtime - An Aboriginal Odyssey
When the Virgin Falls
Kibeho: Original Script
The Kibeho Massacre: As It Happened
Non, Je Ne Regrette Rien - No, I (We) Have No Regrets
The Matter with Karen Mitchell

ABOUT THE AUTHOR

Nigel joined the Australian Army in 1980 at age 17yrs and 2 months, and after completing training at Kapooka was whisked away to the School of Infantry, Singleton, New South Wales, Australia.

He served in the Infantry until injury forced a medical discharge upon him in 1996, after having served in Southeast Asia, 1982; PNG (with the AATPT), in 1990: during the Bougainville Crisis; and in Rwanda, 1995: known world-wide for the Kibeho Massacre which occurred on April 22nd of that year.

Serving in PNG was a major highlight within his career.

He was married in 1999 and has two children.

Stephen stood there, stabilised by his grasp upon the rail of the brigantine as it creaked under full sail, roller coasting along the surface of the sea, breaking waves as it gained in its distance from the calamity of that which had devoured the souls of the men aboard. He was still dressed in the mail that he had fought in, less the tunic, a gift from his wife, and he had long since discarded his breastplate and basinet. And even though the dark void of night had been cast over the sky, like the falling of a blindfold over eyes that burn for the satisfaction of sight, the burning of Constantinople did pave the way for the boat's retreat, the entire horizon ablaze with oranges and reds.

The sparkling of the stars in the sky, where the blaze was strongest, had hidden themselves from all possible view, from the dreaded and poignant disaster below, where the Sultan had secured his victory over the Christians; all Greeks, Venetians, Romans, Slavs, Jews, and mercenary alike. Stephen stood there in his grief, the loss of his one and only true love, gone forever. He, the last of the Templar, and a youth on a journey from that of a child to a man.... but his journey had faltered. Within the wake of fervent need to prove and set example he did leave behind the virtue of his innocence, for it to catch up if it could. Like the wake of a large boat before him, he could see where he had surrendered his youth, as immature as it was, for the splendour of 'cause for action'. His blood had boiled as he fought so strongly, though his mind was leagues behind, gathering the courage to see the fight through... and he knew now that the fight was life itself, not just the battle which had been waged over a few miles of sea and soil.

He had made a vow unto himself, to venture this world both far and wide; to see himself surrendered to the sea like the faeces of an old man left to decompose in the gutter of a city street. He had vowed, in the face of the Lord himself, to do unto himself that which he would not be willing to bring upon someone else. He would die upon the sea, that was his testament to the Lord; no word of living, for his life he did solemnly surrender as being worthless and shattered beyond repair. He thought: God will forever own that which is cast within my blood and bone; never again shall I consider myself a mortal and surrender myself to the whims of man. He was beyond feeling, he was beyond caring, and he was beyond life. Death was his calling, and should that devil-ghost make calling upon him this night, then he would go without protest and allow his last breath to be strangled from the weakened shell he called a body. No, his life belonged to his religion, and although his love was for Jesus and everything he stood for, God was Jesus' father. And for a second, Stephen did contemplate what he was thinking, of how irrational it may have been: never to give in to the whims of man... never to take part in sexual pleasure again. He was a widower, a man with a wife... who, even though parted of this world, was awaiting him, aloft in heaven. He could not, would not, join with another in wedlock.

He was dead already. He was ashamed and saddened by all that had occurred over the past week. An unknown future lay before him now. But be it unknown, be it of little consequence, for he cared not. And he looked again to the sky where several of the stars had become visible, far from the fires that illuminated the night sky over Constantinople, and he did recall the short life he had shared with the one he called Wife.

His dear Clover; how would she see him now, with the knowledge that he have vowed... to end his mortal existence? Her burial at sea had torn him apart from within. And further contemplation: I cannot call myself a man; I am but an empty shell, a cocoon without maturity, and a pestilence of mankind. I am... who I wasn't before. He had no future, but here he stood, awaiting the break of another day, another dawning to bring further torment, awaiting his mind to fester and decay.

How long had he been standing there upon the deck? He had no idea. He had no education on the reading of the stars; no one had tutored him on the secrets of sailing across the sea. He could navigate across land no better.

He looked up at the stars; the shimmering of the night sky over Constantinople was almost gone of its fiery brilliance... what was that? He turned his head in the direction of the sound, something to his rear. At such a time that it surely must be, with the sky as dark and cloudless as it was becoming, it must be reasonably late; he couldn't see how it would have been possible for him to have been standing there alone for any great length of time, but he had. Stephen knew too, that as few as two men would be stationed upon the vessel, their saviour, their victorious brigantine, as it sailed towards the southwest. One man would be stationed to the bow, where the forecastle met the bowsprit, and the other at the helm, where a constant eye could be maintained on the square-rigged foremast and lateen-rigged mainsail.

A two-masted vessel she was, designed for sail alone, the ability for power by oar and sweep left well alone, and steered by a stern rudder. Here, at the helm, the boat could be steered, its rounded stern allowing for short rods running beneath the captain's cabin to steer the vessel as desired: this was a merchant boat of private enterprise, a sea-going vessel purposely built to cater for the commercial needs of the captain, a working horse as grand as a carrack and with the manoeuvrability to match.

He tried emphatically to see into the dark shadows of the boat. He could barely make out the man at the helm, behind the broad triangular sailing cloth attached to mainmast, nor the crudely structured cabin to the rear of the boat itself – which was low set and only several feet high, for it was sunken into the decking to

3

allow the man at the helm good visual both front and aft of the brigantine as it moved smoothly across the surface of the sea. A lantern did burn fore and aft, either side of the helm too; and there it was… a figure looming to the rear. Was the man – or woman – drunk? What need was there to be sneaking about the aft of a boat at full sail, and with such quiet aptitude, a boat endeavouring to be as far as possible from calamity and capture. Turk boats would be after those that had cheated death, the Sultan's orders would have seen to that. Sailors and soldiers alike would have been readied for the capture of anyone who tried a retreat by sea… and land. Mehmet would have set aside a purse of overwhelming extravagance in order to persuade the capture of all of those that had once been a member of the community of Constantinople. The chance of a ransom would also have been a player of mind, enticing many a sailor to forego the promised sacking of 'the City of God' for the chance of riches paid from a secured purse, for captives of all creeds.

Stephen moved his head to the left, stepped to the right, lowered his level of sight slightly and sidestepped again. He decided upon closer scrutiny of the object, and moving slowly and silently towards the rear of the boat did attract the attention of the man at the helm, who did reflect on Stephen's manner of approach but said nothing.

Suddenly Stephen saw a figure of dark temptation playing with something as large as a pottered vase, an oversized chalice for wine, a helmet of war. And it sparked to life, a lantern revealed. Stephen pondered on the formality, which was, to be least implied, without warrant. Why should such be lit? And the man at the helm reflected upon Stephen, he being a darkened figure seemingly looking in his direction, being oblivious to the light that had just come of life to his rear. The lantern also looked quite familiar, but he wasn't sure where he'd seen it before.

The figure of the man… the unknown… he gazed out then, towards the rear of the brigantine, far out to sea where the wake did settle to merge as one with the steady rolling of waves around. And far as far can be, out of the reach of any weapon of war, a

4

signal was received in return. A boat was afloat and following astern, a boat that was sailing in darkness, the only light evident being that of a returned signal. The lantern on the brigantine, on which Stephen stood steady, was then suffocated; the light denied another breath, and then the figure ducked for temporary cover and the man at the helm turned to look towards the rear. He saw nothing, brought his attention to bear once more on Stephen and his strange behaviour, before returning his state of thinking to the sail and the steering of the brigantine.

Stephen crept with stealth a little closer towards the rear of the helm and bare witness to a partial clarity of face, a small beard and shallow eyes, teeth rotten and body hunched forward. The boat far off to the rear then lit up with a dozen lanterns, there, in ones and twos, lit to signal further a field before being extinguished, as was the original signal. The sea was dark but once again.

The Templar continued to watch as the figure of the man moved into the smallest amount of light that was cast from the lanterns of the helm and saw for himself a confirmation as to who was responsible for the signal sent. The features of the man burnt themselves upon Stephen's mind, and his mind leapt into action – as slow as it was. The man must have been a spy, planted to aid those that followed. But the very capture of the brigantine must have been anything but a priority, for if it was desired, the spy could surely see to it that those few currently steering the boat went for a swim amongst the fishes. Why was it so important that a signal be given to their location? Were not the lanterns, at present positioned upon the decking, good enough to provide sufficient indication as to their location and direction?

He shook it from his head. Even at best, those that followed – going by the signal – were unlikely to close the gap. He would remember at first light and bring it to the attention of the captain, but for now he must dwell upon the occurrence, to think carefully about what had just happened… for it was entirely possible that a friendly boat was following, providing secretive protection, for a reason that he did not yet know or understand.

He continued to watch as the figure of the man slipped away and he himself decided upon retiring for the night, to lie awoke upon his makeshift bed whilst the minutes of the night passed him by.

It was only a short clamber down into the hold, which despite its usual cargo of prized possession, was now filled with sacks of flesh and bone. Women and their children, a few husbands amongst the throng. This was what remained of a great city, a few of the meagre that had been spared their lives, on the pure generosity of sailors aboard this boat. There was little room for passengers to move around in by day, let alone sleep by night. Bodies lay strewn upon the bare boards, beneath hastily erected sleeping platforms and pellets that had been put in place from one end of the hold to the other, each and every space available filled with at least one person. Few belongings existed here, for all of those that had clambered aboard under the protest of others, but approved of the captain, had flung what they carried into the sea at the Prosphorianus Harbour, unless such belongings was a consumable of some description. But what manner of food could anyone have brought aboard? Much it seemed. It was quite apparent that many people did accept their fate as though it was drawn upon the mortar within the walls of Constantinople, long before the collapse occurred. Most people had taken the opportunity to have a plan of escape ready to execute at a moments notice, regardless of their faith for the soldiers who stood upon the defences of Constantinople. Good fortune it would appear to be.

Stepping delicately and with much caution, Stephen made his way towards the empty bed – three damn planks of wood set side-by-side, his only burden, his soul possession, a gift from a new found friend, the Teutonic Knight, Lars, the man of no tongue, the legend of a shot when it came to the crossbow, the one and only that had saved Stephen's miserable life.

What light there was in the hold was given by the moon as it commenced to reveal itself upon the horizon, sending a measure of illumination through the few open ports and hatch of the decking above, a moon which was continuing to wane, ever present in the evil it had stirred as part prophecy to the downfall of the city of Constantinople, for it was written that the great city would never fall if the moon was waxing.

He saw his sword resting upon the hung bed of wood and swung himself up into the comfort of his nest, where a blanket had been prearranged, bringing his sword up into his grasp, hugging it close as though for comfort or warmth, companionship or love. He had ventured to Constantinople to fulfil a dream, to bloody his sword, to become a man. He now believed that he had failed, for he was to be forever without his beloved Clover, and as he lay there he finally drift into a tormented sleep, a sleep that was filled with dreams, dreams of death and torture, mayhem and blood, turmoil and defeat. And somewhere in the night so cool, where silence was only broken by the movement of the boat rolling through steadily breaking waves, a voice did lay command over Stephen's senses: He who breaches the bounds of my scripture; he shall be delivered unto everlasting contempt. This is a covenant of your Lord.

Stephen awoke as though shaken by the hand of a heavy man. The voice? Is that what woke me? What does it mean? And the words formed in his mind, as deep as they were, that they would not budge, and would be easily collected for closer scrutiny when he rose with the morning sun.

There were two priests aboard the brigantine, two men of the cloth whom Stephen had seen shortly after boarding the brigantine, by the helping hand of Franco and Lars. He dwelt further on the evening's events, of the day before. One of the priests had given sermon at the ceremony, the captain availing himself to Clover in regards to service, prior to her body being delivered into the sea;

for the two priests aboard were not able to be torn from their current business interest. He'd not heard their names mentioned, but recalled their burden, for they were seen to be inseparable from a chest that they guarded, as though it was made of gold. That in itself seemed nothing more than sacrilege: to carry a chest on board when space was needed for a citizen of Constantinople... wait; he too had committed this same sin, though his was worse. He'd carried the body of his beloved aboard the brigantine, knowing full well that she would have to be delivered to her ever-waiting tomb below the waves; in the least, these two priests still had their chest. But who was he to argue with a priest and his business? They were both a mystery unto themselves; they seemed inseparable, except the first priest, who Stephen did see in quiet conversation with the man who gave signal to the rear... the signal!

Stephen made his way above deck, pushing through – as politely as possible – the throngs as they commenced to converge upon an orderly, whom had been provided the authority to ration all sustenance that could be found. At such a time as this, where calamity, sorrow, and bewilderment was stagnating, in the least, these people, having been stripped of all belongings, gave willingly to a single man who they did not know, all they had. Two meals a day, whilst afloat; morning and late afternoon. None received more than another, child, woman, or man... even the priests and captain were there the evening before, to assure all that the rules of rationing would not be treated lightly by anyone on board the boat. Heavy punishment, lashes to the back, would be punitive enough for a thief over the coming days, until such time that fresh food and water could be secured from ashore. Men needed food and water in order to fight and sail, women to tend the young and sail when men were fighting, and the children of the voyage because they were in their youth, and no one in their adolescence, or early adult years, could bear to see one so young being tormented in ways that should be spared even an animal. But Stephen pushed on, beyond the queue for food, disfigured as it was, for he would forego his meal on this first morning.

He stepped over to the rail of the boat and looked out towards the south, towards the quarter port of the vessel as it approached the strait between Thrace and Karasi, the Dardanelles, 40 miles of sea where the width of the strait was no more than 5 miles at its widest point and well less than 1 mile at its finest. It was doubtful that the Sultan had a force of any strength desirable enough to cause a concern for those making good their escape. The major concern at present was for the lack of a friendly boat. It had seemed, quite apparently, that the captain of the brigantine had waited until the last moment to set sail into the Marmora, for all other semblance of ally had disappeared from view.

Stephen looked up towards the nest upon the mast where a crewman could be seen scanning the horizon all around, and upon the nest a pole, vacant of flag and identity. Shortly though the crewman was making his way down from his post, a look of slight anxiety falling upon his face. Even now, as he made his way down from the platform above, he did look out towards the rear of the brigantine from where they had journeyed. The Templar looked too but saw nothing. The night before he had seen someone give signal to the rear of the boat, and it was his intention to see the master of the vessel... the good captain should be delivered the news post-haste. And as he turned to make for the door of the captain's quarters, the crewman from aloft did push past, infuriating the Templar who thought no good of any other important matter other than his own.

The man pushed on, an odour afloat the sailor seeping into the air as he moved. Stephen was almost brought to convulsion, the man stank like nothing he'd known before: of rotting meat and garlic. And could there be good reason for this? Stephen did ask himself this question. This man's clothing, which hung in rags from his puny body, was stained with the blood of men, his shirt cut into ribbons by the scimitar of the enemy who now resided in Constantinople. Well then, if the picture should be painted as such, then a hero he be, and stench or not he was a man of the earth.

The sailor had flung the door out and practically fell down the short run of steps. Stephen followed without invitation, the door ajar invoking within him the urge to make some good of the opportunity that he had been provided.

"Captain, captain… ah captain, there you be," said the sailor.

"What is it, good man? What service can I provide you?" asked Captain Homer, his name indicating somewhat that his forefathers had something to do with the manufacturing of helmets from iron.

Stephen took the words in his ear as he fell down the short descent, thumping upon the floor, bringing blood to his nose and a little dizziness to his head.

The captain was on his feet in a flash, the two priests rushing forward to provide a helping hand, and the sailor stood back to wonder on the clumsiness and ill manner of one that should intrude on his important news.

"Ah, Stephen I believe?" questioned the captain as he came to his aid, holding out his right hand in support, the cuff of his coat riding up his arm as though too small to fit. "To your feet, sir Knight, for one as bold as you should not be leagued to the floor like a common wife," the smile upon the captain's mouth announcing to all of those around as to his coming attempt at humour. "But even then, a wife belongs to the confines of a strong bed."

"Where this man should be right now," added one of the priests.

"Please, sir Knight," added the second, "a seat for you."

"Thankyou, one and all," said Stephen in return for the kindness, and as explanation was warranted, jumped right to the point. "I saw this good sailor coming to report. I believe I know what news he carries, for I too have something to tell."

"Well, two messages, seemingly of equal importance. Please, men, come sit around the table… my office and quarters."

Stephen got to his feet and was escorted with a delicate touch from one of the priests, the second turning to a chair and seating himself. The sailor stood, deciding that unless directed personally he should remain on his feet. The captain took his position behind the desk, which in itself was larger by one-third as compared to the door of his cabin. Stephen rubbed at his nose and took the offer of

10

an old rag from the second priest, holding this to his sported bleeding.

The captain looked around. "With all due courtesy, I believe we should allow this good sailor to report as he deems so important." The captain looked the sailor in the eye. "Your name?"

"Peter of Pera."

"I'm sorry. Do you have family in Pera?"

"I left no family behind, but a retched dog of useless manner, an animal with the ambition of a goat." He was rambling and eyed each man as they were seated around the table. The captain was square to, and facing the entrance of the cabin, the two priests to the captain's left pushed back a bit from the desk, and the knight sat with his back to the door; Peter was between the captain and the knight. "My time spent above the deck has been as luxurious as any other," and each smiled as he said this, "but just before I descended the mast I caught glimpse of something on the horizon. A boat, Captain; a boat to our stern, and she looks to be carrying the flag of one in league with Mehmet."

The priests and captain looked from one to the other; Stephen lowered the rag from his nose and delivered his news. "I know how it comes to be afloat our rear, following in our wake as though tracking us through the grassy mounds of a swamp."

"Speak, Stephen; you are amongst friends," announced the captain.

"I drew witness to something last night; something which I decided should be slept upon, as all indications pointed to there being no urgency. It is all clear in my mind, and I know who I seek. A man gave signal to the vessel behind... but why they trace our journey instead of intercept us is beyond me. Further still, it numbs my mind for lack of understanding as to why the man at the helm was not killed where he stood." Stephen's eyes had dropped slightly, to look at the floor, and then as quick as a flash, to bring a start to the hearts and minds of all of those around, he looked up quickly. "They must be following us!"

It was then that the 40-mile strait came to mind. The captain looked at the two priests as they sat knowingly. He could draw on his good ability to see into a man's heart… but what choice did he have anyway; they were all retreating; running scared. "Stephen… Peter; may I introduce to you two men of great calibre. Unfortunately I cannot give you their names, for such introduction has not been granted me. These two holy men have something of importance, a chest that contains the very fabric of our religion, something that is said to be worth much to the enemies of Christ."

"A chest?" said the sailor, Peter, as though questioning. He knew, that of the five currently sitting around the table, he was least known about. It wasn't, however, a thing of trust, for it was easy to read the script of one's eyes, but Peter also knew, as did the others, that he would be hung by the words of God if he were to feint his good word or promise.

"Yes," the captain confirmed. "What is more is that they have in their possession a letter from the Emperor Constantine. Without revealing the contents of that letter I must advise of the following: the chest that these two good priests carry, must not, under any circumstance, fall into the hands of the enemy. If such was to occur… I can only hope that it will not. The very thought of the contents of the chest falling into the wrong hands… it's just too overpowering to consider."

Stephen listened with concern. He couldn't help but to wonder if this had anything to do with the dream he had the night before; and it came to him again in a flash: He who breaches the bounds of my scripture; he shall be delivered unto everlasting contempt. This is a covenant of your Lord. The Templar again looked to all and said: "I believe in the Lord's word, and because of such belief must hereby accept sole responsibility for the chest and its contents." Stephen had not realized it, but during his short announcement, had stood up.

The priests looked to one another. The first priest said: "You are Stephen, the Templar knight granted knighthood by the esteemed Emperor of Constantinople. We know of you Stephen, and too have sworn allegiance to the Emperor Constantine." He then addressed the knight. "In this knight is our sanctuary. In you Stephen, is the light of our word… our bond with one of the many sovereigns of religion. The chest must not be surrendered to the enemies of Christ. Furthermore, good knight, it must not be surrendered to any other, be he priest, bishop, or pope. This secret we carry must remain such. We took oath, a bond to protect that which must remain protected."

"I understand," said Stephen and he couldn't be more sober than he was this moment in time: Clover had been forgotten, even if momentarily.

It was then that another voice came to air. "I, Peter, do solemnly swear to act in the good faith that such a mystery deserves. I too will swear an allegiance to the Christ's work."

All stared at the sailor, so young he appeared, but of great character he must be. He had been in a fight so fierce that none could doubt his words.

Stephen thought of the dream that had come to pass him during the night; but it was no dream. "I had a vision last night… whilst I slept." Everyone was listening with baited breath; a dagger could have cut the silence that moment, it being so thick that all noise from the outside had been as though drowned from existence. "He came to me and said: He who breaches the bounds of my scripture; he shall be delivered unto everlasting contempt. This is a covenant of your Lord."

The second priest fell into his chair, the other simply stood there, his jaw open as though trying to catch a fly, a Venus awaiting his pray. "You are truly the one we have been seeking. The Emperor of Constantinople must have worn the inner sight. So strong he must have been not to have allowed it out into the open. A secret that he took to his death." The priest moved towards Stephen, slowly. "This is why you are a knight, Stephen; not because of your skills as a fighter, or a man empowered with the means to be a good leader, good follower, or good ambassador. You are a knight because the emperor saw you in your true light." The second priest continued to close the gap between them. "You are a knight because you have been chosen by the Lord, Himself." And the priests knew of something more, and that was of a short inscription engraved upon the chest in

Aramaic, it read: He shall know his way, upon his quest, travelling far, as bequest, to surrender life, so dear and strong, his way will be painted, with voices strung.

Like a message in a bottle... his way will be strung with the words of the Lord, a map of words which was to provide assistance where required, as though a guardian angel. The priests could now rest a little; their knowledge and quest had now received the support of one lead by the words of the Lord. But there was something more, something else that the priests had not revealed, for beneath the chest, inscribed upon its belly, was the following inscription: Only the purest of mind and body will survive the contents of the chest.

The captain broke the short silence. "Stephen; the one you saw last night? Please tell us more."

And without further hesitation, Stephen provided all ears with the notes of the song they wished to hear, of a man who had given signal to the boat behind. A signal given without any authority, or the support of those in command, a signal meant to draw them into captivity or the arms of death. The captain looked to Peter for his need. "We need to bring this man in for questioning."

"Please," interrupted the first, "if I may suggest... the two mercenary."

The captain looked to Peter again. "Do you know of Anthony and Toran?"

"I do, captain."

"Please fetch them so I may give orders for an arrest."

"No need, captain, I know of the man to whom Stephen has described. If it pleases you I shall pass on your orders directly."

"It does... for the longer he remains free, the more fragile our position will grow."

Peter had departed the group of five, closing the cabin door behind him. The first priest looked the captain in the eye.

"I know what you think, father. They are two good men who fought with Giovanni."

"They are mercenary and should not be trusted with the secrets of the chest," said the first.

"These two mercenary did not abandon the defence of Constantinople until ordered to do so; they were amongst the last to run."

"I would still insist on secrecy," said the first, "for it is against our better interest to have too many ears made wise of the chest and its contents."

The captain added, "I do not even know what contents the chest holds. I pledge my life to Christ and His father; I pledge my good position, granted me by highest station, to provide you with assistance, but still I have no information… other than what you offer."

"We understand your curiosity, captain," said the second. "But you have not been chosen."

"Is it simply curiosity to me; to want to know what it is that I fight for?"

"Nevertheless, the chest will remain secure… at least until the key can be found."

"A key?" asked Stephen.

"Yes, Stephen," replied the first, "a key of wood: cast in wood so that it may be used but a few times, for an overuse of the key would render it useless. A key so perfectly manufactured that even now, after so long, moisture may have rendered it obsolete."

"Why such a restriction?" questioned Stephen.

"To limit its use; to ensure the chest remained sealed; to secret the contents. If the key is broke then so will be our spirit. An overuse of the key will see to it that it will be used no more. The chest will become locked forever."

"In fact," interrupted the second, "the only way to open the chest, without the key, is to defile the very existence of our religion and its beliefs, for it would have to be broken... smashed beyond repair."

"Where is the key?" Stephen looked from the priests to the captain.

The captain fidget slightly, leant forward with his arm extended in a quest to relieve his thirst, grasped the tumbler in his hand and drew it to his lips. He drank and then placed the tumbler down. "It is said to be secure and in good hands."

"Where?"

"Not far." The captain looked to the priest. "The exact location is not known to me, but somewhere on the island of Káros, Southeast of Náxos."

"There is a temple there," explained the first. "A small dwelling protected by some knights from Rhodes. We shall deliver the chest to the location of the key. Once the chest has been secured, its contents can be revealed. We can then decide upon its fate."

From an Anatolian port they had originally sailed, aboard a Turkish mahon of little but striking proportion, a galleass of 25 oars to each side, quite capable of running down many of the enemy boats. It was propelled primarily through its use of oars, but did have mast and sail as a secondary means of propulsion. It carried three masts and had a forecastle and aftcastle, and was steered by a stern rudder, of which its wheel was situated to the rear of the cabin. It was 150 feet in length and required the logistic allotment of 100 men to thrust the vessel through he water at top speed: which was maintained through coxswain beating upon a drum. In almost all cases, that could be scrutinized, the crew of rowers were provided for by slaves, convicts and prisoners of war... alas, so hard it was to get a trusted crew, for most would spend the best part of any day shaking in fear and chained to the oars. But the crew in this case was provided for through ingenuity and greed, for men were fuelled better via the offering of gold and pillage than through terror alone.

The oarsman were exposed to the open air, for the mahon itself was open, though decked at the bow and the stern, and along the centre of the boat it was well stocked with provisions and arms. But for the attainment of speed the vessel had been lightened by given up all formality of protection, and the sides of this particular mahon could not be raised in order to offer protection to the crew.

Currently the mahon was running off of the charity provided by the wind, for the power of the oar was not currently required. The Turk in his greed was more after salvage and ransom, than the complete destruction and sinking of an enemy boat: at least until it had been ransacked of all its wealth and its women raped.

Ah yes, a good raping was what lingered upon a soldier's mind, to tear at the under garments of a wench on heat, to smell the sweat of her body as she perspired in terror. Such were the glories promised a soldier in the servitude of Allah, that it was favoured most amongst the crew that were now on the tail of the brigantine ahead. What ransom awaited them? What plunder would there be for them to take for themselves, to hold in their grasp, to clench so dearly, so closely to the heart? Few of the crew, in actual fact, knew the truth. Gold and coin, the wealth of a good ransom... ahhhhh, and the rape of a good woman; yes indeed! Few knew the truth of the trophy, the reason and cause for their being, the circumstances surrounding their chase at sea. Few knew of the chest and its secret, but the orders had been given. What man would surrender the opportunity to sack Constantinople? None! It was absurd! No man in his right mind would forego the three days of pillage, which had been promised him... without good cause. And good cause

17

had been provided. For the sanctity of all minds a story had been hatched. The crew had been told of the gold aboard the boat to their front, of the strategy that was to be played out. Yes indeed – and beyond all thought – they were going to be very rich men before the week was out.

Their commander was known as Abu 'the strangler', for it was said that he suffocated the women he raped: pleasure wasn't for a woman, so therefore, if enjoyment was received by the woman then death she must meet... and what woman wouldn't be satisfied by 'his tormented', the manhood he kept locked away between his legs, awaiting a release from the dark of the trousers that held it at bay; like the leash of a dog, it restrains its venom. He had only now raised himself to the waking of the new day, the second of many to come, he was sure of that. But whether the chase was two days or two hundred he would not quit until his task had been completed.

He traversed the short climb with ease, exit, the cabin now behind him, and looked briefly over the crew: left to right and left again, along the entire length of the mahon's nakedness. Most of the men were sleeping below deck, in its lowest of quarters. All was to his satisfaction, all seemed to be in order. He then peered up to look at the platform high above, to the lookout above the deck. Abu recognised the man immediately, it was Ibrahim, one of his best men, a sailor of much experience who was worth twice that at sea as he was on land... and even then he was a most potent soldier.

"Ibrahim," shouted Abu. "Ibrahim!"

He went unanswered, but all around turned to see what the cause of the shouting was, although in reflection, it was not a voiced command or scolding, but carried a note of friendship, of happiness.

Abu cupped his hands together around his lips and shouted again: "Ibrahim!"

Ibrahim looked away from the bow and down to the aftcastle, seeing his commander standing there with his hands cupped around his mouth: Abu with his hands cupped, as though ready to strangle. Ibrahim would tread carefully this morning, he knew of 'the strangler' and his reputation, and this morning Ibrahim had nothing but bad news.

He descended the mast to make his report, to provide news on the situation, direct to the commander, the man Abu, whom considered all to be his friend… yes indeed, friends for the feeding of cannon, fodder to be employed as he saw fit. Ibrahim preceded quickly, the palms on his hands running over the coarse rope of the rigging, the pores of his skin not a stranger to rough treatment, for they had been hardened through many years of hard fighting. He descended his post most professionally… quick and with ease, landing foot strong upon the deck of the mahon, turning erect and with a smile, looking to Abu above him. He scampered along past the oars and up past the coxswains seat and drum, to stand before Abu, looking him in the eye.

"Ibrahim. Tell me good friend, what did you see aloft that will bring party to my ears?" Abu lifted both of his arms, clenching Ibrahim's shoulders between his palms (the strangler), a show of affection short lived, and then they dropped to his side. "Speak."

"News on the Christian vessel is good, Abu. They sail directly ahead, for the narrow pass; but…"

"But what?"

"I am sorry, Abu; no good news this morning on those that accompany us. I received report last night… as you did, that the signal was received from the brigantine and then passed onto the port, starboard and stern, exactly as ordered."

"You have no sighting of our second in command? No sighting of the other four boats which accompany us?"

"No, no sighting at all. You heard yourself, Abu; that signals were received from the other boats… but… they are gone."

Abu's look of optimism soon passed, and a worried and stern look commenced to develop upon the cold lips of the 'one that strangles'. He turned side-on to Ibrahim and lifted his gaze to take in the ocean around; the few birds that seemed to float upon the breeze, and the sky as clear as the night had become in the early hours of the morning. Abu had all intention of closing the gap

19

between his small armada and the Christian boat. There would have been no escape for the Christians. Then, as they exit the pass, and into the Aegean Sea, he was to pan his force out into an extended line prior to enveloping the hunted on all sides, it being impossible for the Christians to escape. But now... now he had nothing. And Abu looked up, a change to his facial expression coming of age, for the plan that had died had given rise to a new.

He turned abruptly. "Ibrahim! We shall speed up, close the gap between the enemy and us, and when the time is ripe, before we enter the Aegean, we shall board the brigantine with grappling hooks and planks. We shall have our victory, but before the original pledge. Go now, order for more speed." And his voice rang out loud. "All listen hard to the words I now speak! Get to work as though for Allah himself. More speed is what we need; more speed! Prepare to set oars!" turning to Ibrahim he gave a command. "Fetch me Ahmad Kadir and Mouley Bakar. Have them in my cabin before I have time to pour myself some wine."

"Yes, Abu." Ibrahim set to the ready; scurrying to the task he had been set. The two commanders, of lesser warrant, would be given the invitation immediately – or was that an 'order'?

The captain had poured refreshment for the priests and Stephen, tumblers of wine: this was no sacrament so healthy portions were provided. All drank but one. The captain looked at Stephen, the Templar sitting there.

"A tumbler of my finest, grown in Constantinople. The taste must be sampled in order to grasp the true character of the grape, for the fragrance alone tells but only half the story."

"If I am to fight for what I believe, if I am to protect the chest as I have so sworn, then a clear head I must keep; above all I must remain vigilant, and in command of all my senses."

The priests put their drinking vessels down in unison. None other could give such praise to the Lord than the words that had just been spoken, and no sooner had they both returned their hands to their laps then the commotion outside did reach their ears.

"You are all aware that torture may need to be performed." said the second, as more of a statement than a question; and if it was one thing that the first knew, and that was of the second's love for torture and the truth. All present looked at one another... All now stared in anxious wait, towards the entrance of the cabin as the noise drew closer and grew in ferocity. Muffled sounds were then heard, commands given by one, or both, of the men who escorted the man responsible for the lanterns that night... a hand over the devil's mouth? An order for the traitor to cease with his physical demeanour was then accepted, for little could be heard but a cluttering of feet upon the deck.

The door suddenly swung open and the traitor was unceremoniously pushed into the confines of the small cabin, to fall in front of the counsel that awaited: "In there you slime," said Anthony, his open palm giving an almighty push, the traitor falling to his knees before looking up with pity in his eyes.

The traitor wore a black eye and shrivelled hair, long and to the neck. Dirt covered half his face, blood the other and the look of dismay upon his face began to evaporate. From far beneath his breath, in a cavity of ill-will, he summoned his courage and spat out a ball of slime towards the captain.

"Why you, filth dog...!" exploded the escort.

"Wait!" commanded Stephen, for Anthony held in his left hand the hilt of his short sword, which by demeanour of movement did wish to discipline the traitor. "A blow to the head will do little for us at present."

The captain wiped the slime from the tabletop. "Check his bonds; have him kneel before us."

Anthony did as ordered and Toran turned to the gathered crowd, reaching out to receive the traitor's possessions, before turning again and placing the belongings in front of the captain,

21

for all to see. The captain eyeballed the crowd as each and every sailor, or so it seemed, tried to peer into the darker confines of the cabin.

"Close the door." And his order was carried out. He now looked the prisoner up and down, a traitor as was not denied. Guilty by pride, guilty by acceptance, guilty by witness. Guilty he be and for such a finding… death. "We know of your escapades… of your willingness to do us all harm. We have spotted the galleass which follows." The captain stood as all watched. He paced around, looking down upon the head of the traitor: the traitor little amused kept his eyes to the front. "You know, no doubt, that death awaits you." He paused to let the word sink into the head of the man on his knees. "But death can come in many forms. Is it to be quick or slow?" The captain placed his left hand upon the shoulder of the intruder, as though a friend: consoling his victim. "A quick death would be much preferred… by us as much as by you; I am sure."

"Death is my calling, my calling is God, and God is most powerful."

The comforting hand slipped from the shoulder. "Will it be a quick death?" asked the captain.

The traitor in tattered clothing looked up at the captain and allowed a wry smile to caress his lips. "I shall see you in the fiery furnace of hell before submitting to your charity."

Stephen knew of torture, had seen it once, a long time ago. "You should save yourself the torment and trouble," said Stephen, "for we know much already."

"Then why do you see the need for torture?" the traitor's eyes connected with Stephen's. And Stephen thought: this is a most wise man, for he understands he is to be tortured without such words parting our lips; and then again, how else were they to get the information.

The captain continued: "Who else of you is amongst us?"

"That shall be my knowing and your demise," replied the guilty.

The captain continued back to his original position and stood there, looking down in disgust, seeing no alternative but torture. "So be it."

Ahmad Kadir and Mouley Bakar were commanders little sought, for their prowess in delivering a finished product; for with any task, it was always tarnished with something that had spoilt, and in most cases, due directly to their individual or combined incompetence. So why should men of such little calibre be chosen for the task of netting a great prize, a prize that was in fact beyond the imagination of even the scholars of Mehmet's inner circle.

Ahmed Kadir was expendable, as too was his companion Bakar, and due solely to this expendability was often chosen for errands of great worth and longevity… it was also widely known of his barbaric attitude towards anyone of his current opposition. He was extremely strong in regards to his virtue and greed: for ransom and gold. If a coin was to be had then Ahmed was your man. Courageous not, but what courage does one entertain when commanding over a servitude of scimitar wielding vermin. The sailors he commanded were nothing more than rabble, sloths of a grandeur not usually accepted within the Turkish ranks; but their willingness to kill… to torture their victims, to kill women, children, and babies at a glance – and not feel the worse for it later. Never gamble with your life, but take company of these men and life is what you will be short of. Lustre was rare, sodden cloths and rotting teeth were bountiful. How could such a coward of the high seas, as the one just described, be so able to tend a flock? Two men of particular form, muscle bound giants with wit to spare, educated in many tongues and scorned for their knowledge on all things to do with war. Abdullah and Muhammad, two men whom were but dog's on a leash… Mehmet's dogs of war. Directly to the

23

sultan they answered, and his bidding was for them to command this venomous crew of faeces through one who had tested the tide of his patience. To death Kadir would have been marched, but for favours the sultan owned the sister of another in his league. Rather a delicate, political situation this was. Yes indeed; Abdullah and Muhammad would see to it that command and structure remained set in place.

And then Abu's voice could be heard, mixing with the noise of the wind, an order for more speed and something about 'square the oars'.

It is here, upon the open deck of the mahon, that Abdullah and Muhammad can be seen by Ibrahim as he made his approach, Ahmed Kadir having walked off to relieve himself over the side of the boat at sail. Abdullah was playing 'dice-n-cup' upon a rowing bench, with several members of their band, when Muhammad announced rather poetically that the roller of the die had cheated. It was in fact a false accusation, for the branded cheat had in fact done nothing wrong except have a bad word to say on reflection of their task. Such mutinous talk was unequivocally forbidden, and all of the crew knew it. None of the crew wished to be disciplined by Kadir – though in fact it wasn't a discipline from kadir, as so much from the sultan himself. Abdullah and Muhammad ruled the roost, and their persuasive attitude and command over Kadir worked wonders when so far from the rectitude of a port. Kadir also knew that to receive good praise from the two giant men was to receive good treatment and exercise from Mehmet himself.

Muhammad stood abruptly from the blanket strewn across the bench, thundering loudly his accusations, pointing a finger down upon the head of the man still kneeling, the smile upon the face of the soon-to-be vanquished diminishing as though like a clap of thunder. "You have cheated for the last time. Your dice is crooked, and the other is loaded with lead," and indeed it was, but only because it had been planted by Abdullah.

"No! NO! You are wrong!" And as quick as the words had failed him, the quicker a blade did penetrate his lung from behind, Abdullah delivery the deathblow. No sooner had the accusations

24

been laid and the man was being prepared for an unceremonious displacement into the waters of the Marmora.

Abdullah pulled the blade from the flesh, letting the body slip to the floor. "Syahid; get this filth monger from off of the deck and carry him to the port. For bait he will be used... though God knows, probably bad in taste."

"Yes, Abdullah; immediately." And the body was carried away before it even had the chance to fall completely to the decking, amongst the oars, and ropes and other things found upon a boat.

Abdullah looked at Muhammad. "Such a dislike I had for this man that to waste my words on him would be an insult to Allah."

"My friend," Muhammad said to Abdullah, nodding his head in the direction of the messenger Ibrahim. "I would hazard a guess that we are needed."

"Indeed," agreed Muhammad, and looking to the other three sitting around the blanket upon the bench gave further advice. "I hate cheats; but I dislike those who believe that uttering mutinous words is a mandate for sanctity in heaven on death. Ahmad Kadir has a good head for tactics, and will be worth keeping alive... do you hear?"

"Yes Muhammad," the three said in unison, and picked up the die and blanket, departing without so much as an exhaled exclamation of disagreement.

Muhammad quickly turned with a smile and warm greeting, extending both arms in order to show his affection for Ibrahim, "Ah, my good friend. Allah be praised for treating you with the respect you deserve, for this morning you look wonderfully refreshed."

Both parties released the hug of greeting then and Ibrahim looked Muhammad in the eye. "I seek your commander; Ahmad. More speed has been ordered and oars are to be set. As coxswains it would be in your better interest to make-ready."

"Kadir... ah, indeed a good fellow who not only looks to our health, but also keeps our minds fed with sanity. You look after us far too well." Muhammad was known widely for his sarcasm, even

25

at the best of times. "Our comrade in arms is attending his need right now."

"And what need is that?"

"The need for privacy," and he winked.

"There are no women on board to speak of, so you must be referring to his going for a shit," Ibrahim thought himself rather witty at this, for he smiled.

"Such lovely to hear words of wisdom from a scholar as yourself, Ibrahim." Muhammad pointed, his eye planting the burning look of ridicule into the head of the messenger. "He is over there."

"Thankyou; I bid you good day." Ibrahim departed, walking with great stride over the open floor of the decking of the boat as it rolled to-and-fro, towards the place where Kadir could be found, ignoring the laughter as it exploded from the mouth of Muhammad, like the burning vapours of sulphur from the pits of hell, waves of desecration exploding from a volcano.

"Muhammad," said Abdullah, once Ibrahim was out of earshot. "Be careful."

"You think me afraid of that weasel?"

"No, but I call for caution."

"You always call for caution. In actual fact, you call for as much caution as I yearn for the touch of a good woman."

"Ah, yes. I too yearn for the opportunity to have my way with a woman. And we will both get our fill when we board the Christian boat. Not long now, my brother,"

"No, not long at all," said Muhammad, looking around to ensure no ears were invading their privacy. "I think we should retire to the hold; our good friend Syahid should be reporting shortly."

Several planks had been retrieved from below deck and placed parallel to each other upon the captain's table. The wish was to have the man tortured elsewhere, but with a cargo of old men, women, and children, what could one do? Wasn't it bad enough that torture should have to be exercised?

A small vase of oil sat upon the table between the traitor's legs, and an open pan of burning fuel – wood, coal, and a little fat, positioned just out of reach at the base of his feet. The coals were red hot: and there was a poker there too, its handle sticking out like a big plump, long thumb. The instruments of torture were simple here. A red-hot poker did well in purifying the mind, in relaxing a knotted tongue; and the oil, well enough for roasting the underparts of the feet. But the poker was best, for it created greater levels of fear within a man.

The traitor lay naked.

Both priests stood, one to either side of the traitor as he lay upon the planks, his arms straight, tied at the wrist, and then the ropes were secured to the table legs at that one end. His legs were parted a fist's width apart, a block of wood positioned between them just above the ankles. His feet were also bound, the loop of the rope placing inwards pressure upon the legs, the block secured and unmoving. It took little for the imagination to realise what was about to take place.

With the priests were the two men, Anthony and Toran; they would do well to serve the holy men as required, though the need to now restrain the traitor was little needed, for he would be unable to move.

Stephen was not present and nor was the captain. Stephen was where his bed had been laid; resting as best he could whilst the torture took place. Such actions should not be the will of man to enact upon another, even if such a man was a traitor. The captain was to the other end of the hold, giving a short speech to the cargo of flesh, assuring them as best he could that little fear should be dwelled upon. Stephen could hear well all that was said.

"And what if the galleass should catch us?" asked a frightened soul, a woman of her later years, a child under either arm. The children were not hers, but had given aid to her in Constantinople, as she now gave comfort to them.

"The men will see to the galleass. But you women must be prepared. You must all help where you can. The children must stay below and out of harm's way. All of the rest must play their part in the fight that is sure to come. Women can help with the sails; they can help with reloading arquebuses…"

"Fire crossbows," yelled a female from somewhere towards the back of the crowd.

"Anything to prevent the Turk from boarding our vessel," continued the captain. "Should we be boarded… that will spell the end of our retreat."

"A retreat!" yelled another. "You speak as though we are to gather our forces and fight again, to simply withdraw to another defensive position."

"We are heading to a place where salvation can be attained. Some of you will know of the island of Káros. A garrison exists there, strong enough to repel those aboard the galleass. The long run to the island will be easier to manage than anywhere else within the Aegean Sea, due to our advantage with wind. I know well the wind patterns of the Aegean."

"Why not Lemnos?" someone in the crowd questioned.

"Euboea." The crowd was becoming agitated.

"Chios." Anywhere but Káros, for that was so far away.

"Please, good people." The captain had his hands in the air now, holding at bay the mounting fear. But the truth could not be told them. "We have to consider much; for one thing, the manoeuvrability of the galleass and this good brigantine; their comparative speeds, the sailors who sail them. The wind will be in our favour for a move to the south. We must venture to a place

28

where we know exists a garrison of good men. Káros is the answer."

"But what are we to do in Káros? What—"

"And I am the captain!" he was losing patients. "You good people are under the protection of this boat. We sail for your better need. I would not subject you to capture any more than I would subject myself to torture," and he remembered where he had to be, his calling. "You must organise yourselves into groups fitting the task to which you are most capable of rendering service. There are men here that can help you in your choosing. Every able-bodied person must play his or her role in the conflict that could fall upon us soon. When we enter the Dardanelles, we are of limited movement. If we are to succumb to the Turk, then it shall be here. It is a long journey. You must all prepare for battle." He then turned to a shuffling sound: Stephen was standing at his side. The captain needn't introduce the Templar, but gave of his knowledge freely: "This man, you all know. He will sort you; he will give you knowledge where it is lacking, and the spirit to continue as we do…" and he looked upon the gathered throng, "but courage you do not need, for you have all the courage one could ask. I know you shall all serve the Lord well, as you have already done."

The captain turned to Stephen before departing, giving a slap of encouragement and a smile to boost morale; signs that the Templar knew were of trust and knowing, and on his expedient departure Stephen did take the floor. "Each of you here has a special gift or talent, even if you know not of such a trait. Each of you must search deep, look into your souls; it is there where you will see the measure of your vocation."

"My father was a fisherman… I helped him several times when the sea was wild," said one woman.

"And I shot a crossbow once," said another.

"I am a master boat builder," came an encouraging word.

"You all have a gift," continued Stephen. "Lars? Lars my good companion; where are you?" a hand was seen to shoot up from the rear. "Lars," and Stephen addressed the crowd, looking over them

29

all as he spoke. "Lars: the beast of the Teutonic." A murmur from the crowd. "That's right! You see him there! Standing firm! He is but beyond doubt the greatest marksman one could ever expect to meet… with the crossbow I say." the crowd looked behind, heads bobbing left and right to catch a glimpse of this man of iron. "I tell you good people, a tale that will astound you. That man there, Lars the Teutonic, has but no tongue," gasps were heard; more shooting glances. "Cut off, I tell you, to prevent from revealing the true defensive strategies of a castle he helped protect against Muslim invaders… that's right, cut off by action of his own hand." The crowd was flabbergasted at such heroism, such courage: but of course it was all a lie, but warranted. "Seek him and teach he shall, and within minutes you will be a master as he." A few persons moved on the spot where they stood. "But wait! Of sailing you need but another, someone skilled, someone as good with a rope as Lars is with his crossbow. Most of you know Franco…. Do you not?"

"I do!" shouted one man,

"And me! Over here!" came another.

There courage was growing, their spirit, their confidence, their very inner strength. These common people were the answer to a prayer.

"Then let it be said and done. If you seek knowledge on sailing, go to Franco; the master Lars awaits your good attendance… and I shall teach the sword."

The crowd was bubbling with excitement and divided themselves as equally as one could expect, between the three men.

A woman came up to stand beside Stephen. "I am a nurse. I know a few good people that can fill my needs."

Stephen looked the woman in the eye and smiled, a tear beginning to form as he recalled his beloved Clover. "Good woman, you choose your own ground and take what supplies you require. Even if the men have to fight naked, you shall have all the cloth you need."

Ibrahim skirted around a few barrels fastened to the inner deck, roped and strapped, around the centre mast and other wooden boxes of cargo, before coming face to face with Ahmad Kadir. So nearly did he bump into the man that he picked his arms up to cradle his carelessness by holding Kadir's forearms and took a step backwards.

Kadir looked up as he finished putting away his manhood and did his belt up fast. "If I did not know better, Ibrahim, I would say that you meant to reach out for my privates for companionship, rather than my arms for stability."

"Excuse my haste, but Abu wishes to see you in his quarters, immediately."

"Ah… I see… and what good news is it that forces Abu's mind to conjure up a meeting so early at dawn?

"It is to do with the Christian boat."

"Ah, yes… the Christian boat… always the Christians," said Kadir, talking down to the deck before looking up and finishing with what he had to say. "We would do better without the vermin, Ibrahim. The worse for wear I have been since resigning my life to the sea," and the subject changed as abruptly as it had started. "Chastity it is, which can never be broken…"

Ibrahim seemed lost of words.

"Look you…" Kadir scoffed and pointed. "Down there you fool, upon the water, swimming through… no, dashing through the waves."

Both men looked down, over the side of the mahon at full sail, a porpoise swimming alongside, enjoying the chase.

"A fish."

"A porpoise, you uneducated vile of filth. What manner of man are you that cannot tell one creature from another?"

31

And indeed it was, quite dissimilar to a dolphin, by few characteristics and visual sign. A small toothed whale it was, growing no bigger than 6 feet in length. Its triangular dorsal cut through the waves as it swam, carefree and without concern. "So rare a sight as this may never pass your eyes again, good Ibrahim, even if a life at sea is all you come to know."

"Little concern it is to me. A fish is a fish. If it fills my plate and the hole in my stomach, then fish it is for the eating."

Kadir considered the words. "Eat? EAT? You don't eat such creatures. This is majesty of the waves, a feature to test the senses like the... the.... Consider the appeal of your favourite dish; such appeal brings joy to you, to sing out loud."

"My favourite dish is sauce of garlic poured over a steamy hot plate of fish."

Kadir gave the man to his front a stern look and then shook his head. "See it, Ibrahim. Look at the porpoise as it swims. It feeds on fish too... just like you."

"Its oil is to a lamp, like its flesh is to my tongue."

"And what manner of tongue is it that can bring such a majestic life to the dinner plate?"

With that spoken Ibrahim pointed, for another sailor, up front and aloft the forecastle, did suddenly thrust down a harpoon that penetrated the porpoise's head. It let out a faint shriek of horror in tribulation, and was quickly reeled in with much joy enveloping the one who had caught it.

"That man, soon to become my best of friends, has the tongue... and I have the plate."

And with that Ahmad strode off quickly, for he wanted nothing more than to be rid of the defilement and the collar that he wore in regards to his current station.

The captain returned to his cabin in time for the commencement of the torture, the scene to his front rather demoralising. He had sailed many seas and an ocean, had sailed into ports right across Europe. There wasn't a language he hadn't heard spoken, all colour of man-flesh having passed his sight at one time or another, but nowhere on this earth had he yet found the stomach for the word 'torture'… and now he was condoning its very use.

The men to his front went about their business, finishing up with their individual tasks. He was surprised to see so few instruments of pain upon the cloth of white, which had been laid upon a chair. There were a knife and a brush, and a smaller container… containing what, he did not know. The traitor was laying quietly, not a word passing his lips. He was looking to the roof and beyond, praying from within, asking Allah for forgiveness if he should be so cowardly as to relinquish the information that he carried – and little that was. He was praying for strength, for salvation, for a quick death, even if such was to be the uninvited.

Toran looked up, standing to the right side of where the traitor lay, beside his head; Anthony was to the right. "We are ready to begin, Captain."

All eyed each other then, for a brief second. The captain gave a nod, it being received by the priests whom stood at the victim's feet.

The first priest took up the brush from the cloth of white and dipped this into the vase of oil that lay between the victim's feet. He withdrew it, and as though painting the bare boards of a boat in dry dock, did paint the feet of the traitor quite thickly.

The first priest put the brush back into the vase, his robe rubbing, seemingly by accident, against the traitor's feet, a vast majority of the oil being removed. The captain saw this and was about to give advice when the priest continued: "I shall tell you now what is about to fall upon you. Your feet will be roasted and the poker we are to employ will scar you from head to foot. We also have a quantity of powder: it will be amusing to see the effect of it as it burns upon your flesh. If you answer our questions now, then you will go to your god unscathed. What is your decision?"

The traitor said nothing; just laid there, his lips murmuring to himself a prayer for salvation. The traitor's mind had readied itself, as best as possible, for the effects that were about to be delivered unto him.

The priests' first assignment was to make the man of guilt talk quickly though bring as little pain as possible to him. Only in this way, with a slow built up of pain, was the victim to be assured that a compromise could be reached. If the priests were to escalate the pain to its highest degree, then the man laid upon the planks could well be pushed, both mentally and physically, beyond reproach. The last thing the priests needed was a gibbering wreck of a man, whose tongue wagged a song of a different tune to the one they were after. But also, how best to ensure that the truth was being spoken. They knew a little of this villain, and thankfully, he did not know what they knew. They would call his bluff, pass on to him false questions with known answers. The traitor too, knew much of the science of torture, understood the formality and torments, false questions and answers, of the questions that would be asked over and over again in order to try and prove that he was lying. But there was something else, something that both priests and the traitor knew, and that was that even if he talked and gave willingly to the questions asked, the priests would still continue with the torture to ensure that they were indeed receiving the truth. The traitor, indeed, knew as much about torture and the proceedings, as did the priests – the priests however, did not know that the traitor knew as much as they. There might well be a compromise, but it would only come after much pain had been delivered.

And so begins the lengthy task of torture.

Mouley Bakar was the other that Ibrahim was seeking, and he was found below deck, where it was customary to keep the convicted and prisoners of war, during times of rest between turns at the oar; he was enjoying the comforts of a late morning. Bakar had no caretakers as such – not like his good friend Kadir – but he did have good reason to command as best he could, the foot soldiers under his command. His one and only son, a youngster of just several years of age, was being held at the point of a blade. Bakar served in order to preserve his son's life; but what was such an impoverished life to one like him? His son was to remain in a cell for the remainder of his life… or until Bakar, himself, had served adequately. And who was to say if he'd served well enough to secure the release of his son, and why was this life so important? One of the soldiers under his direct command was a spy… he'd been given this much information, but he didn't know who it was… the identity of the spy had been kept from him. In order for the release of his son to be secured, this man's life was to be kept intact. Such pressure made him a tough leader, but over cautious. He was crazed with paranoia. As for his son… he cared little for the sack of shit he called family, but his son was the last heir to the family in which he had been married. Yes indeed, on his son's release, Bakar would become a very wealthy man. But Bakar was no fool. What if he was to find his wealth during this very voyage? Did he really need to return to Mehmet for the gift of his son's life, hence the gift of the fortune that he desired? But what of the spy? And what if there was more than one?

Ibrahim approached Mouley Bakar as he washed himself, splashing a little water upon his face, rinsing the look of sleep from the creases that formed his brow, mouth, and cheekbones. A few scars, tiny in comparison to the ones he wore upon his body, stained his right cheek with a blemish of red. But it wasn't so much the scarring that turned women away from the man, but his personality.

Mouley could hear the steps of approach as Ibrahim closed the gap between the two. "And what does our beloved commander have for me this morning, good Ibrahim?" he said, not even tempting to look up.

"He wishes to speak with you in person; on matters of great importance."

"Great importance is it?" Mouley took his shirt, wiped it across his face, and placed it over his head and onto his body. "Every morning our esteemed commander has some important matter that needs my undying attention." He began the task of tucking away his garment and picked up his sheathed scimitar and belt. "Come Ibrahim... surely you know something. Tell me, what is in the air this good morning?"

Calm and sarcastic: nothing new for Mouley. "The brigantine is ahead, we have no other friendly boat in sight, and... well... the remainder must rest with the imagination."

Mouley stopped and looked at Ibrahim. "Do you have the foresight? Can you see for yourself," and continued to finish dressing. "Or do you lack the imagination of that which you speak?"

"I only come to request your attendance; as ordered."

"As ordered... of course. And I thank you most graciously, good Ibrahim, for your task is now complete, and mine just begun. You may run away now and report to our commander that I come panting like a dog on heat, with tail between legs."

And off Ibrahim did run, allowing the sarcasm to drop away.

The captain stood back and allowed the priests their prestigious task of communication with the traitor; for the interrogation was about to commence.

"Tell me of the other boats: how many are there?" asked the first priest.

"I can tell you no truth."

The second needed no signal, he commenced quite calmly and with little effort, to build of the fire that had been given birth. He poked the coals with his iron stick, a little flame licking its wrought features. In and out he poked, and it was then that the finest of gasps did escape the traitor's lips. Before now the pan containing the fire had given off nothing more than a little warmth; but now it had well and truly started to build. The radiant heat was spilling outwards and heating up the oil basted upon his feet.

"It is never too late," said the first, "to adhere and repent."

"Repent. Not only do you wish me to sell my friends to their grave, but now you wish me to repent. What shall I repent to, father? Ah… I ask you… to what should I repent?"

"You have joined brethren of infidels, to bring calamity and disheartenment to our great religion." The traitor scoffed. "You bring upon your very breath the devil's own work of words, voicing his sacrilegious verses and blaspheme openly."

"It is you," said the traitor, "who blaspheme." And with that the red-hot poker was pulled from the coals, as warmed as it was, and was dragged slowly across the stomach of the restrained and guilty victim. His screams were exasperating, to say the least. The captain shied, his arms crossed in front of his body, the two guardsmen held down the shoulders of the traitor, and the two priests' eyes battered not a single shudder.

"Speak now and you can prevent further pain!"

The burning sensation... no... the sheer agony, the uplifting excruciation, the burning torment which penetrated the traitor's body as the poker was drawn across the flesh and returned to the fire. The skin continued to bubble up, the first priest employing his skill well, and the fluid from the wound being contained. The smell of burning flesh hit their nostrils.

The traitor calmed down momentarily, catching his breath, the heat building slowly upon the soles of his feet. And before the traitor could compose himself completely, and without warning, the glowing poker was drawn once again across the body of their victim; and the screams did penetrate well into the confines of the cargo hold, where children cuddled their mothers – the mothers who were too old to fight or sail a boat – and men looked up momentarily, as though able to see through the boards of the brigantine that partitioned them from the open air and scene above.

"How many boats follow in our wake?" asked the first priest again.

The traitor was gasping now, in much pain; as much as he had ever encountered in his life – as a free man or as a soldier.

"How many boats? Answer this question and you shall have a drink of water."

"Your water will not be enough to extinguish the flame that burns me this moment."

The first took the iron from the heat and applied it again, this time a little lower, just above the groin, dragging it skilfully across the flesh in order to prevent the skin from rupturing. Screams again filled the air around the confines of the cabin, screams that penetrated the very soul. The captain shook the smell of burning flesh from his head and Anthony entertained a wry smile.

The priests were in for a long day; they both knew this. Answers they needed, but such answers: would they aid them in their defence against those following? It would be true to say that regardless as to the numbers that followed, those aboard the brigantine would have to prepare the best defence they could muster; but what also of other traitors on the boat?

"How many boats follow?" his exasperation was building; he was growing tired, and yet he had just commenced. If the man tied to the table top knew not the answers to the questions being posed, they were going to end up with a dead man, torture being endured all day. If the traitor knew the answers then he could well receive reprieve, even if of minuscule compensation for that which he'd already suffered.

"You have but a few marks upon your body. I am sure you will wear them well... but will it be through pride, judgement, or hatred, that your memories of this day will be rekindled after death?"

The penetrating heat upon the soles of the traitor's feet commenced to build quite affectively. The constant feel of burning underfoot could not be extinguished from his mind. He knew for sure that this day would be his last on earth.

"Does such..." he gasped, "a question... help with your... cause?"

"I am the priest," said the first. "I shall ask the questions. How many boats?"

The question went unanswered. The traitor was forgetting himself, losing his mind; all he needed to do was answer a few questions, which were unlikely to help the Christians cause in any case. The first took the iron from the pan; it was now glowing white at the tip, and the priest ensured that the traitor could see this. The priest averted his eye contact with the man on the table and applied the furnace-hot iron to the inside of the traitor's thigh. Screams immediately erupted from deep within him, and continued unabated as the poker was dragged skilfully across the flesh of his leg, down towards the knee, and up again.

The poker was withdrawn and the convulsed body of the traitor stopped immediately, relaxed completely, not a taunt muscle existed anywhere. The man's chest heaved up and down, but he was unconscious.

"Toran: some water, quickly!" urged the second. Toran turning for a bucket filled with water. "Let us wake this man whilst the pain is at its worst."

The first priest could see the conviction building within the other; he wouldn't be stopped.

Toran grabbed the handle of a ladle and withdrew it, splashing its contents unceremoniously over the head of the traitor. He awoke, gasping... his guts screaming for oxygen and a release from the pain that burned across his body and up the inside of his leg.

"How many boats?"

"Five... boats... all manned... manned...." He lost consciousness again.

"Toran," the first indicated for another ladle of water with a signal of his head. The traitor burst out again with further gasping. How many men on board?

"I... I..."

"HOW MANY?"

"One hundred...and... twenty."

There was silence: it lasted but the time it takes a whore to secure her wages within her undergarments. "Who is in command?"

"I... don't know."

The priest was on a winning note, and wished to keep the upper hand. He lashed out convincingly with the iron poker, to the same thigh as before. The screams attained this time around were the worse yet to fill the vacuum of the cabin.

"The Strangler... Abu, the Strangler."

The knowledge was tucked away into the backs of their heads, for further information was required. The second priest then voiced a question, one that he was interested in hearing the answer to. "And of others amongst us that spy as you do: how many and who are they?"

Ahmad Kadir and Mouley Bakar entered the small cabin, Abu seated to their direct front. He was sipping on some wine, a luxury of office that was not permitted the men who worked beneath him. It was no surprise to see him sitting back in the lap of luxury – as good a luxury as any could expect, in particular when cast out to sea.

"Ahmad, Mouley, please, come and sit so that we may talk." His display of rank and confidence didn't impress the two men, any more than the belief in their faith gave them the right to strike out at a woman, with heavy and clenched fist; but still, it was done; and so, with chins up and chests puffed out each took their position in front of the desk with a degree of pride embellished upon them. They stood there, the two, waiting to be spoken to; and then it came. "I have been recipient of bad news, as is normally the case when commanded by chimpanzees and eunuchs. No one can expect full flavour of choice to overwhelm a palate when ones tongue is wrapped in an iron cloth... and this voyage of ours has been more than a shackle when it comes to orders; but still I follow them as a good commander does." Abu stood, his hands interlocked, placed behind his back. He turned away from the two men then and faced the open porthole at the rear of the cabin, looking out at the wake of their boat at sail. He turned abruptly and faced the two. "Precise orders have been given, but incompetence on the behalf of those that follow, have seen to it, quite clearly, that such cannot be followed, as they are nowhere to be seen."

Ahmad looked to his side and Mouley did the same, looking each other in the eye, temporarily lost in the avalanche of words, before returning their attention to their commander.

"Yes men, I see your look. Understand do you, the orders I have been given? Why, you haven't even seen them, yet as commander I am left with a choice. Specific instructions were gained by me as an advantage to this great voyage of ours," and the two in front could only wonder as to why the word 'great' should be spoken, "and orders followed shortly after." Abu sat, looked left and right upon his desk, and stood again. "Orders to remain linked with others to our port, stern, and starboard, before gaining upon, and then surrounding, a boat full of slave and ransom. But where are the boats; where is this great armada of support and power that was promised...? gone. Like the wind which casts a thousand clouds to sail the skies into oblivion, to sail until released of its purpose. Are we to be released of our burden? No I say." Abu was silent long enough to draw a few breaths and looked at them standing, though they were advised to sit; and then he continued. "Please, draw in a chair and seat yourselves." The two men did as requested and in silence. Abu sat too. "The orders I passed onto you are a direct reflection of those I did receive from higher station, and as such would normally remedy precise action to ensure they were fulfilled. However... we can no longer comply, as we are now sailing upon the sea, behind a Christian boat of riches, and not a friend to speak of; and not only this," Abu drew a deep breath, "but a traitor... yes, that is what I said, a traitor. A traitor aboard the Christian boat did give signal to us last night, at a time when the sands within my timepiece did herald, whilst you were both asleep in your cabins of refuge. I received the signal personally before organising the other signals to be delivered our boat's stern... and so on." Abu fell silent, he had prompted enough, or so he thought. He awaited a response from the two men, a question that did not come. He continued: "you may ask yourself why such a traitor didn't press for a slowing of the boat to our front, and... I am sure you are intrigued. The boat to our front is heading for a location, which we yet do not know. The boat is to be followed until such a time that the location would be revealed to this; traitor. Ample time was to be provided him, and then we were to strike. With five boats to our side, we were to board and take all for ourselves, to be washed in the riches found aboard, in both flesh and gold; all that is, except a chest of secrets."

The men's jaws dropped in unison. "A chest…?"Ahmad asked.

"…Of secret's?" finished Mouley.

"Aye. I thought that would grasp your attention. But alas good men; good leaders that you are; for the chest is not of our belonging. It is for the sultan to do with as he sees fit. We have but been granting the sacking of the Christian boat, as though it was a suburb of Constantinople, a floating city where 3 days and nights of pillage will be granted."

"You deem to declare the right to sack and pillage a boat as though it were a city?" asked Mouley.

"I do. Your men will be permitted to do as they please, so long as the chest remains unmolested. The women may be raped at the good humour of your men, and the gold and ransom split equally… or as you see fit."

"This chest must have great value," concluded Mouley. "Good enough perhaps, for me to be granted my freedom and my son's release."

"I have the power to grant just that, but you and your men must fight as though empowered with the vigour of five, for no friendly boat is nearby. The men beneath you must be willing to sacrifice themselves, if the need arises."

"They must be granted special favour, above and beyond the sacking you so openly promise," added Ahmad.

"And so it will be granted, to all the men… once we have returned to safe harbour of course."

"And to our orders, Abu?" questioned Ahmad.

Abu stood, the other two followed in action. "I have ordered more speed, as much that can be mustered. I wish oars to be set, within the time it takes me to piss. We must gain on the Christian boat; now instead of tomorrow, or the day after that. We must strike whilst the manoeuvrability of the Christian boat can gain but little to no advantage. We will attack whilst sailing down the Dardanelles. It would be in my interest to fight at first light, allowing us good wind for our closing of the distance tonight. Men can do without sleep: all will remain stationed at oars. We must employ 80 men at all times stroking the surface of the sea... 20 at rest should do it; and the marine detachment shall remain on call to duty and must be provided the opportunity to rest, where rest can be granted. The brigantine is weak and manned by old men, women, and children, so nothing more than a handful of marines should fill our need... nevertheless, rest they shall be provided. So go now, and give your orders. Ready yourselves on this eve of fighting to come, for tomorrow you will be given all of the freedoms your hearts so desire. If a friendly boat follows, we will leave it in our wake. The spoils of war will be ours alone. Go now... and if we need to speak again before last light, it will be for me to bring discipline to bear upon your shoulders."

Both of the lesser commanders stood without further word, and bowed to Abu before turning on their heels and departing with purpose.

The door to Abu's cabin burst open and Mouley let roar: "Boabdil, Abdar, and Hamed, bring yourselves to me! NOW!"

And from Ahmad: "Abdullah, Muhammad, bring me your ears! Men... good men around... prepare for battle, for by morning's light your scimitars will be caked in Christian blood!"

Weapons, ammunitions, and other supplies, were scarce to say the least, but where good supply the Christians did lack their spirit was overflowing.

Lars had lived many years, more than half his life, with no tongue in his mouth. He had learnt well to deal with the accustomed remarks and cold stares, the manner in which mothers would shield their children from such a monster as he. But for the years of torment that had been felt and rubbed in deep, came a foreboding insight, and he was a natural when it came to reading

44

the minds of others around him. He could read the look on a face as well as he could hear their tone, whisper, or malice. He could read their walk as well as a touch or a slap. He could adjust himself readily to any situation as though born to it.

Lars stood to the front of his small congregation of seven. Two women in their 40's, a man in his 70's, three boys of their mid-to-late teens, and a girl of eight years. It was to the girl he first looked. She was bewildered and calm, looking up to him as though lost to the world of sanity, a lost sheep in search of its flock. She had lost her innocence and was looking for comfort, but here, where Lars did stand, was only one type of comfort... and that was the closeness drawn from a crossbow and its quarrel. What a pitiful creature of beauty, what innocence of life this was, to be wasted upon the defence of the Christian boat, where life would soon prove to be put out to the slaughter. Lars knew as any other, that this girls life depended on her being able to defend, being able to shoot at will, being able to kill without second thought: for if she did not, then she would be raped as any other women aboard this boat, raped repeatedly, until she did die from the loss of blood... and even in a circumstance as this, it is hard to comprehend, but even in death, the Muslim pirates would still be slapping their groin against hers, grabbing what sexual pleasure they could as she lay void of life. Be it for them, they did not care. Be she dead or alive mattered little. The soft touch of her skin would be to their delight, and rape they would, and without repent, regardless of how cold her skin did turn. Yes indeed, they would have their way with this little girl, as though she was a sheep in the fields of slaughter, to be molested as well she deserved, for she was a Christian upon a Christian boat, and as anyone of the Muslim faith would deliver, she would be taught of her faults in life and religion.

Lars offered his helping hand to the girl of eight, a smile upon his face providing support, his delicate touch appealing to her in many ways. His touch was a friendly touch: very warm and open. He was her friend and father, brother and king. To the little girl, Lars was everything, and to see her lightened smile, as she looked up into his eyes, did bring a tear to one of the women who watched from the side.

Lars knelt down beside the little girl and put his arm around her, bringing her in closer, dragging her across with his left arm. And in his right he held the crossbow, balanced perfectly upon his open palm. Lars looked to the weapon and then into the girl's eyes. He held it to her, bringing it closer to her body, to place the stock of the weapon against her shoulder. He meant no harm to her then, but grunted and bore his teeth, for she wouldn't relent to the lesson. Her smile disappeared, and Lars grunted again, more forceful this time, pushing the stock of the weapon into her shoulder. She sobbed gently but did her best to hold back her tears and gave into the instruction being delivered. The moisture that built upon her eye clouded her vision and her face showed the torment that she felt upon body and soul. Lars grunted once more, forced again the stock into shoulder. The girl took it and looked down the groove upon barrel, seeing first hand what it looked like to peer down the length of a crossbow. Lars stood up then and grunted once more, indicating another man from behind to come and relieve him, the only other aboard the boat that was a professional when it came to firing the crossbow. Lars relieved himself then, of the lesson at hand, and strode away quickly, to hide his face in a dark corner of the hold, to shed a tear that couldn't be held at bay. The floodgate was open and he would rid himself of this burdened pain, this inner stabbing-of-the-heart that he felt. He would rid himself of this anguish and return afresh, for these people, regardless of age, had to be taught a few lessons on self-preservation: for the last thing Lars would accept, was the repeated raping of a child still of her youth.

Franco stood atop the deck; women and children of age, swarmed around him like bees after a honey pot. To work the sail and rigging one had to have strength and courage... no less courage does one need to climb the mast to crow's nest, any less than one needs to fight a janissary. "It is a different courage I tell you. You know yourself, deep within your very hearts, whether or not you can scale the rigging of this brigantine, to place yourself within the confines of that wooden palisade... a wooden box from where you can peruse... at your leisure, mind you, the seas around as you sail upon its waters." And Franco felt the confidence building within and paced the deck like a good tutor does. "Why, what do I see before me? Young Master Andrew. Why, boy, how old do you be?"

"You know that, Mr Franco, sir," answered the boy.

"Tell everyone here, announce it so they may take heed."

"Ten years, I am ten years, this year."

All around smiled at the display of confidence. "Well, ten years and full of pride; ready to pull of the rigging I bet, and you too... yes! You lad! Come here, tell all around your name."

"John, my names John – I be eleven years, this year."

All gave to a round of applause, smiles set freely upon the mouths dirtied during the withdrawal from Constantinople. "Well, I never," exclaimed Franco, now turning to address the crowd, "never in all my years of sailing, did I see such grandeur as that displayed by these two young men here before us today. Great hope they have instilled within me this very moment, the very hope, no... the very knowledge that the fight to come will be won." And the gathering slowed in their applause, for they were but meagre old women and men in need of revitalization, and they all feared the fight. Franco could see... could feel the very fabric of

47

that which held them together stretch under strain. He drew alongside of and sat upon a small barrel, open palms placed upon his thighs, elbows held high. He got up again. "We stand alone good citizens. We alone must help ourselves in the fight that draws near. The larger vessel that follows from behind has set extra sail, a galleass from behind which will no doubt catch up to us before we reach the Aegean Sea. It is up to us to ensure that martyrs be made of those that follow. It is as important to them, to be remembered in death, as it is to us, to be benevolent in life. Look to these two young men, both have many years to look forward to, and both are willing to fight for their right to live. But they also fight for you. We fight for each other. But our skill at fighting is not as sound as it is in those that seek victory through the sword. For victory we must set upon the tasks that are to be surrendered by those that relinquish their posts during the fight to come. We must all be able to replace the sailors, when the sailors take up arms against the vermin that follow." Franco then indicated the two boys coming of age, referring to them, that the others may follow their example. "Such confidence, such marvellous displays of courage that I ever did see before. We must all learn the ways of this boat like we know our own arms and legs. Each rope is a sinew; each mast is a bone. Your eyes are the lookout, your feet are the sea; the wind is your stride... the manner in which this brigantine was built; that is the essence of you all, the spirit that must surface and be clear for all to see. This boat is our last refuge... we have nowhere else to run. We can no longer retreat."

Stephen stood in front of the gathered men: half a dozen in their latter years. There also stood amongst these volunteers, ten women, five boys of around nine years of age, and three girls of between six and eight. He first wondered on his approach, a speech that may be appropriate to the situation. He was a man, no doubt, but one so young... could he muster the essence, that which was required to forge these refugees into fighters? What choice did he have?

He stood there in silence, looking over the small congregation, wondering on his ability to teach, and their ability to learn. Old men and women; young boys and girls. The sailors aloft the decking, shifting sail and tying down rope... they had a degree of knowledge on fighting, had to... in order to keep at bay the boarding of pirates.

Old men and women: what were they that he should trouble himself to teach? These people couldn't have the power to inflict damage upon a foe. The galleass that followed was higher out of the water than the brigantine, at forecastle and aftcastle – this was against them. Those that followed were better trained – in actual fact, any training, regardless of how professional, would be better than that about to be taught these poor sacks of flesh.

It was then, as though in a flash of light that the voice came to his ear but once again: Greater love has no man, but he who surrenders life with good cause. You will not see decay when delivered unto the Lord; and there shall be no prejudice comparison between servant and master, for no one is above the Lord. This is a covenant of your Lord. And all of those around Stephen stared in bewilderment, for their teacher seemed to be reflecting on some unknown apparition, his facial features aghast at something mystical, his mouth agape as though in awe of an empowering enlightenment. The people looked to one another, wondering on the sight before them all, of Stephen, as the gaping hole beneath his nose did close, and a smile commenced to develop upon his face.

Stephen looked to the men: "Do you believe in compassion, do you believe in love?" and said it with such a radiant smile that those that listened were compelled to answer.

"I... I believe in the love between a man and a woman, the strength that it holds," said one man.

"I shall say that a parent's love for his child is greater," said another, for he knew of parenting and its responsibilities.

Stephen gathered his thoughts in the silence, the sound of the sea voicing its opinion, waves slapping against the hulk of the boat as it cut through the turbulence created by movement of wind upon surface. "Two have answered; one for marriage and the other for God." Stephen gave to reflection. "Is it not God who bestows his love for us, better still, our love for Jesus and His love for us. God sacrificed so much by giving us His only child, to be slain upon the cross like a common dog. Yes indeed, that is love. The love Jesus held for us all, this also called out, for he gave His life in order that we may be forgiven." Stephen looked to the children, so sweet in there early years, so different when older. "Little girl, so pale and tall, what is your name?"

"I am Catherine, sir," answered the six year old.

Stephen looked behind, took a spear that had been leant against the side of the boat. He held it out to her. "Do you know what this is, Catherine?"

"A spear..."

A woman gasped and then quickly covered her mouth, shocked to think that Stephen would wish the girl to defend the boat against being boarded.

Stephen stood erect. "The child is right, it is a spear. And now Catherine, another question for you: What would you do with this?"

"Enough!" voiced one of the men, the Templar's gaze distracted. The teacher then scolded, but without his voice being heard, for the look within his eye told all around that there was more to his words than question alone, and that his voiced opinion should be heard without drawing false conclusion in reflection to the movement of his body.

Stephen smiled and looked at the girl again. "Do you know its purpose?"

The girl took the spear and held it in her hands. "I can do this!" and thrust the spear out at the rail of the boat, as though into the flesh of a pirate. Stephen stood as further exclamation was received from the gathering, more from surprise than not, for the action of the girl spoke for itself: she was willing to fight.

"To the gentleman who prefers the good love for a child," and Stephen recalled what John the Hospitaller had told him days before, whilst in the defence of Constantinople. "Would you accept that this child, although not of your own in blood and virtue, be yours in faith and honour? Do you honour this child? Will you treat this child as your own? Would you protect her with all of your heart?"

"I can accept... No! I cannot accept responsibility for that which is not mine."

"And of the gentleman who preferred the good love of a marriage, the bonding of a man and a women: did not such a bond see to the deliverance of this child?"

"I cannot say... I know not the parents."

"It is not a direct question, kind sir," continued Stephen. "But rhetoric of belonging. Did not Jesus, and God, believe that all men were of his body, belonged of his flesh. Was it not spoken? Father, forgive them, for they do not know what they are doing."

"What is a belief in religion to do with this child?" voiced the man so fond of love in marriage.

"It is our duty to perform our belief. This child has shown merit. She has told us that she will do what she can to prevent the boarding of the infidel. In return, I should hope, that you will do as much by protecting her from the devil's lust for pillage and rape. Should you not give your life to a good cause, as Jesus did give His? I ask you not, kind sir, to throw down your arms when confronted by the enemy, but to call upon all of your spirit to defend this child's very innocence. If you throw your life down, like common garbage is thrown into the sea, then you will not reap the reward of everlasting life. I am... we all are, asking you to give your life for this girl, as Jesus did give His life for you. This girl is one of yours, and one of mine; we are of the same flock... we are family. It matters not of your wealth or good station in life. Jesus does not prejudice between servant and master, and neither should we. Even if this girl were of darkened skin, she would still be ours to protect. Look inside yourself, sir… all of you, look deep. We are all one and the same, we are all God's creatures. This little girl has already sworn to protect you: will you do the same in return?"

The one so fond of marriage spoke: "And what is it that we must do; for the fire in me can hardly be rekindled, and the youth of those that follow in our wake will deliver the edge of their scimitar in such a way that I stand not a chance of parrying such a blow."

"What is your name, sir?"

"I am Niketas… I was born of Constantinople," said the 40 year old.

"No," said Stephen. "You were born of God, and Jesus is your Lord and Master." Niketas said not a word but accepted the chastisement for what it meant. "And you… yes… the man who would see the bond of his family strengthened through the love for his child."

"I am Rainald," said the man. He then appeared to puff out his chest, ever so slightly. "I am of 51 years… and I am still full of fire."

"To be full of fire is not good enough, for you must ensure the flame is delivered. And Niketas… if you believe you will be struck down by the scimitar, then that is what will happen." Stephen paused for a short second. "You must expel all of your energy within, to fight as you have never fought before. I shall say this to all of you now: if you should collapse to the floor of this deck, then it shall be through sheer exhaustion. You cannot feint courage of strength through training, you cannot prove your worth through strenuous exercise with sword or dagger. But the spirit you display when the fight does come, that is what matters. It is here that we must train ourselves. Yes… I can teach a little on protection; the tactics that we must employ to keep the infidel at bay; but the victory will only be won through the exuberance that you deliver when the time is ripe. When a man comes to you, to fight you alone… what do you do? Niketas?"

52

Niketas wasn't sure as to the answer, but something within spoke for him. "I must fight like there is no tomorrow... that is the only way to beat the beast."

Stephen smiled, walked up and down in front of the gathered throng. "Is he right? Is he...? No, don't answer," he held his open palm. "For I can see that none of you will know the answer, none of you here can give me the correct response." And the small crowd was dismayed and hurt; they couldn't believe the unkind words that had been flung in their direction... and then the Templar finished with: "For you are all too generous and proud; you are all too merciful. I shall tell you what you should do." He looked Rainald in the eye. "When Niketas is confronted by the devil, you my friend, Rainald; you will come in from the side and push the point of your blade into his body, and as he withers upon the deck, another of you will fall upon him, and dig his heart out with a dagger."

The crowd were silenced... mostly; but one gave way to a dry-reaching, sickened by the explanation. And there, amongst the crowd, was one that stood silent and smiled. Stephen looked to her then and smiled in return and the gathered were silenced. All stared then to the one responsible for domineering over the class: it was the little girl. "If this one, being so pure, can convey to the actions required, then you ALL can follow the example. We do not fight with rules. Rules are for the merciful, for the proud, for the strong. You must all become weak and surrender to the ways of cheating. The only way to win this fight is to be as low and vile as those that fight us. You must surrender your conscious motives, you must not give into charity... you must NOT give mercy. This is your path to victory, and on this path are the actions you must embrace. To win against filth you must become filth.

Syahid thought: A chest of secrets. What secrets could lie within the confines of a chest at sea?

He shook the thought from his head and continued listening, stooped as low as he possibly dared to hope, over the lip of the stern of the mahon. He had already – although in a precarious position – been paid off well. Eavesdropping on the commander, Abu, was daring enough… to do so in full light of day was pushing the limit.

Again it thumped within his head: a chest of secrets. He listened more on the conversation being undertaken between, Ahmad, Mouley, and Abu.

What? Three days of pillage. 'The strangler' was offering everything. This chest of his must be worth a mighty sum; if only the situation could be manipulate to best suit my needs.

Ah, ha. Mouley is going to receive special favour, and… what's that? All of the men will receive special favour… more speed… no sleep… by morning's first light… time to vacate my position, for to be caught will see my head bound to a log and displaced by unfavourable means.

Syahid slipped away quickly and quietly, his listening post above the rear cabin's porthole having served him well… better than even he could appreciate.

He took off in urgent need, though careful not to arouse suspicion, for as he came around from the rear of the cabin, Mouley and Abdullah did burst from Abu's quarters, their voices filling the air with commands.

He moved quickly towards the entrance of the hold, a segmented portion below, which had been partitioned and made ready for use by the officers and other official men, and down into the darkness where his eyes would take time to adjust.

Syahid looked left and right as he approached Abdullah and Muhammad, having been running the errand on which he had been sent, the errand that he now sought to report. Both Abdullah and Muhammad stepped into the confines of a shadow as they saw him approach, a corner within the hold that hid them well from any prying eye. No one else was around when Syahid came calling, and this was to their liking. Fleeting eyes drift here and there, ears open to all manner of sound, ready to scrutinize anything out of the ordinary.

"Syahid," said Abdullah. "What did you hear?"

"Abu sang well and gave orders to pursue the Christian boat."

"So early," stated Muhammad.

"Abu sees no reason why caution should be displayed, for the others that are with us, are… not with us."

"We know this already," Muhammad was tempered. "Tell us something we do not know."

"Abu has ordered that we should gather speed and capture the Christian boat. He has also pledged three days of pillage."

"Pillage a boat over three days when it can be done in far less than one; absurd," said Muhammad.

"But something more… something which will be sweet to your ears," continued Syahid.

"Speak the sweetness, before I grow sour," said Abdullah. "Wait!"

A noise of clatter, something dropped down a rung of steps. Someone was entering the hold. The three in hiding slunk back: ensuring the security of the shadow they sought did cover them well.

It was Abdar. He was rummaging through his belongings, muttering away to himself, something that couldn't be heard. And then an exhale of satisfaction came from Abdar and he ascended the hold as quickly as he had arrived.

"What did you hear," reiterated Abdullah, signifying that it was all clear to continue with the information.

"There is a chest…"

"A chest?" asked Muhammad.

"Let the man finish with his report," said Abdullah. "Go ahead Syahid, before someone else comes calling."

"Abu is after a chest, a chest of secrets."

"Secrets," again Muhammad interrupted.

And Abdullah interceded, clearing his voice.

"I am sorry," and Muhammad waved him on.

"A chest of secrets exists, a chest that is for the sultan's eyes only. It is of great worth. Mouley has even been given the promise of freedom from duty and all of the men are to receive special favour... once the task is complete and the chest is secure."

"What worth does a chest hold that the sultan should be intrigued by its very existence? It must be filled with gold and title, jewels from across Europe, and grants of distinction," said Abdullah. His greed was being met, the cavity he held within, for the better consumption of riches, was getting its fill.

"Syahid, nothing of this must pass your lips," said Muhammad. "We have been close friends for so long that I believe trust has developed enough for us to draw parley of distribution... much wealth there must be for the sultan to be entangled in, what appears to be, insurmountable interest." Muhammad touched his finger to his chin. "I believe I can draw also, upon the trust of three under my influence. Boabdil, Abdar, and Hamed."

"Do you really think such is a good idea, Muhammad?" asked Abdullah.

"Indeed I do; with you, Syahid," and he looked him in the eye, "and these other three, we stand to attain much power. What is Mouley to us? He is as expendable as the rats I chase from my blanket each night, and the ones I kill supping on my breakfast each morning. The fool thinks a spy is watching him... such pity I must draw... what a pathetic wretch he is. If the sultan thinks I am to return, to be treated by him, as the dog of a servant, then he needs to think again. But, Ahmad is different. I believe that with a little persuasion that Ahmad will come to our banner. He owes his niece nothing, although in fairness he does owe his life to her existence. What do you say, Syahid, Abdullah; do we pact? Are we in agreement to form a union between us with, Boabdil, Abdar, and Hamed... Ahmad will be nothing more than a puppet. Others will be happy to follow, once they know the structure of command."

"No, Muhammad," answered Abdullah. "We must be seen to have control, to maintain coercion and command."

"And which of the two, of you and me, shall be seen to be in command?" replied Muhammad.

Abdullah thought on this. "You are right. Two in command will not do."

Syahid felt a little left out. He was as good a man as Abdullah and Muhammad. Why should he not be in command, or at least in communion with the conspirators? "I too, agree with this." Both other men looked at Syahid, who in return felt the stabbing of eyes and curses fall upon him. "We are three, not two. Ahmad will do well to command... he is a good tactician. He can serve well. If we are to band together, with just a handful: what is it to us that they know, that Ahmad only commands as a puppet?"

"So it is agreed," concluded Abdullah. "We allow, Ahmad to command... due to ability of strategic importance only, and we... as three... shall be his masters."

"Let us shake on this agreement," said Muhammad, and the three did agree.

Peter looked upon the table of the captain's quarters, his cabin of refuge, his office and sleeping quarters. He had entered half way through the torture of the traitor, but now it was complete. The priests had the information they had sought, and the captain was satisfied, to a certain degree, that a defence would now benefit from the information gained.

The two mercenaries, Anthony and Toran, had commenced to clean away the tools of torture, the hot iron was put out in the bucket of water, and the ladle affixed its place upon a cornice. The priests said there last prayer and the captain sat in his chair and poured a handsome dosage of wine... that which he had prescribed himself, to ease his nerves. As for the traitor, he lay upon the planks, scars numerous across his body. The stink, as well as the mess, was also horrendous... as could be expected, for his feet had been roasted well. The traitors left foot had been so mutilated that the sole of his foot had been burnt half off: such is a trait of torture. As for the traitor... he was dead. No chances could be taken on his lying. The truth had to be known, even at the expense of another human being. But he was an infidel, and with such a label came misfortune. He was the devil in worship, a beast of malevolent worth.

Peter had never seen torture before, and now that he had, wished that he had not. The tormented screams of the traitor would live with him forever, the smells of burning flesh reside with his nostrils till his dying day, and the instruments of pain would remain forever inscribed upon his mind.

And then, in the back of his mind, something shook him back to reality, awakening him from his fever-pitched guilt and apprehension.

"Peter, do you hear?" continued the first priest. "Get for me a blanket, enough to wrap this carcass in, for even with the devil he worships, a burial at sea he will be given. For his contribution of information, he will be forgiven; for his devil worship he shall be burdened... in death, like the torture he did submit to, with sheer agony, for he did commit to false worship."

"Yes, Father, I shall see to it," and off he scampered, to the task he had been provided. He exited the cabin door, sped past several men who were standing around talking amongst themselves. He caught a brief glimpse of Stephen to one side, where lecture was being administered, to strengthen minds and obedience, and Franco to the opposite, further towards the bowsprit.

He continued to the hold, where he brushed past another and continued to his place of quarter, where blanket was secured under his armpit. He then turned to make his way back to the priest but fell upon Lars as he moved, bumping delicately into the idol... this brought the knight to a temporary frustration before he summed up a benign look of disregard.

"Good knight... sir Lars... I am aghast at my carelessness. My esteem apologies, good knight." Peter's cluster of words were well heard by Lars, who stood his ground and shook the ignorance from within, and with the helping hand of the man who had astonished him, brought to head the finishing touches of composure. The Teutonic let out a little huff, but gave no indication that he desired to reprimand the sailor. "I beg your forgiveness."

Little forgiveness there was to offer, for Lars felt little troubled by the occurrence of Peter's action – in particular now that he realised that such a foolish collision was far from being on purpose. The knight looked at Peter, realising that the good soldier was aboard the brigantine well before he, and having such honour, was more than likely more astute as to the provisions of the boat. Peter could see lustre develop upon the man's eyes and wondered as to the thoughts that lingered and festered upon his soul, it was then that Lars – with a grunt – held up a quarrel within his left hand. Peter looked the missile up and down, and then to the eyes of the knight himself.

"Ah... I see. You want to know if further supplies are at your disposal?"

Lars smiled, "Ooooo," and nodded.

"There is, sir Lars. I saw provision wrapped in canvas, marked with the stamp of a symbol representing an arrow... but... that could have been for a bow; does it matter?" for Peter didn't know the specifications of the crossbow that Lars did carry.

Arrows for one were not arrows for another. Seldom was one made universally, where it could be employed with more than one type of model. Thought Lars: A boy, even if immature and of unfledged wings, must surely know as anyone, that it is best to have arrows made specifically, where they are manufactured with specifics in mind, where they are different from one weapon to any other. Arrow points were just as significant – depending on the task and desired effect. Lars nodded.

"Well, maybe I can show you... yes?" and Peter felt the excitement well inside him.

Lars looked at Peter and nodded, amused that the boy seemed to think him illiterate, for his tone and action of words mounted argument that Lars was nothing more than a retarded beggar woman of little disposition.

"Please, sir knight; this way."

Lars followed, his lesson left far behind, and his thoughts now entwined around the boy, Peter. Here Lars was being lead along like nothing more than a dog off a leash. "This way, sir knight. That's it. Not far now."

Lars considered the triggers within his companion's head. Even if the knight were of six years of age, he would find it hard to believe that he would be treated in such a way... but this was the law of being misunderstood. It was in fact this very action that brought people to the conclusion that Lars knew nothing of fighting and should be shuffled aside in order to fetch dry powder for arms, water for thirst, and food for celebration. Be he, he thought, the most misunderstood man who did walk the face of the earth. Then he thought further still, of the question in regards to arrows. It was only due – primarily – to Lars' unquestionable perfection of his art that he believed each brand of arrow did harness special powers, which would be reflected when employed in the specific weapon strung for such a missile. Peter on the other hand, was still a boy (by comparison), and had not founded a particular skill... therefore, he would be quite satisfied and apt to employ an inferior arrow with a particular choice of strung apparatus – even if such a weapon gave poor performance due to the poor choice of quarrel or arrow.

They finally arrived at some cargo strapped upon the centre of the forecastle, where indeed, Lars did meet with a little surprise. The canvas packages, resting aside the stack, were unwrapped carefully, and although not of much use to the crossbow that Lars did carry, were of good quality. Not only this but a large quantity of bows was also in existence: the only other type of weapon that coincidentally enough, did suit the skills of the Teutonic.

Lars beamed a smile that fell from ear to ear, and the joy he felt in securing such a find was only heightened by the enthusiastic handshake that Lars gave Peter, and the slap on the back that would have knocked a well-rooted tooth out of the head of many an old woman. Peter smiled too, happy to have been of service.

Abdullah and Muhammad reported to their station, the stern end of the open decked galley. Along the length of the boat, on both sides, sailors had taken their positions, oars had been thrust out and men took their seats upon the benches of work. So old was the mahon that imprints of the men's backsides could actually be seen, scars of indented buttocks, a signature of the boat which read character into the very planks that moulded the mahon and spoke of its spirit. An old relic of war still at sail, that's what she was, a beast... not of burden, but of a sacrilegious trend, for this boat had seen to the misery of many enemy... and for all of its years at sea, had seen as many enemy boats sunk, due primarily to its builders and the double planked bow of superior construction.

Abdullah sat upon the coxswain's throne: and although not a seat of power, was most definitely a seat noted for its distinction. Big men they were, Abdullah and Muhammad, yet never in their days had their palms brushed faces with an oar or a sweep. Muhammad sat comfortably to his left, a pallet of blanket and straw drawn up by Syahid, sitting just to his rear. This bed was the station for the relief, where one would rest and the other would beat upon the drum. They were quite different from the sailors, in all respects. Both Abdullah and Muhammad had worked together for many years, and this year was the first that they had worked on a mahon – or any other boat for that matter – which did not have slaves or prisoners of war manning the oars. This was a fresh idea, from one of the high officials who worked under the sultan. Why beat a slave to death, hence, reducing your power at oar, when condemned men could be provided a promise of reprieve if they did stroke the sea well. There was also the promise of ransom and rape – not bad for a convict. Many a convict erupted into smile when advised of the possible payment: the opportunity to stroke the bare flesh of a woman, and all they need do was to stroke the sea with as much enthusiasm.

As for Syahid, he was their companion, their runner of errands. If Abdullah or Muhammad thirst for water, Syahid would go running; if they hungered, he would fetch an appropriate dish. As coxswains they never went without, for their task was of upmost importance, and Syahid was to see to their every wish. In fact, Syahid relied upon the generosity of Abdullah and Muhammad, as they depended on him for the much-cherished privy information. He was most definitely a spy like no other.

Abu approached the open floor of the deck and looked down upon the men... in their two's, forty men to each side of the mahon, the oars were taken hold of and pushed forward in readiness to receive that illustrious first drum beat. Abu smiled. He was happy this day, even with the poor news of the others in his small armada not being anywhere in sight. There would come a day, he told himself, that he would see to it that precise orders accompanied any task, and if such orders were not obeyed to the letter, than heinous punishment would be the just reward. Promotion: such a cleansing word that offered great gifts of station, where one could enjoy the fruits of ones labours, even if struck to sea for years on end. It was well within his grasp... a promotion to reflect his abilities, and when such a promotion was received he would ensure all orders were carried out as required.

All was at the ready. Coxswains were standing by, as too was Syahid. The oars were manned; Ibrahim was standing by to press home any order given him by his commander. Ahmad Kadir stood at the ready, to the side and between the coxswains and rowers. Mouley Bakar was standing upon the forecastle, his marines stationed in pairs around the mahon in readiness to receive orders (such were the delights of discipline and parade, where all would maintain their post until all formality had been concluded, and once they were under full sail and power of oar they could be stood down to maintain a rostered piquet). Boabdil, Abdar, and Hamed, stood by Bakar's side – group leaders of good sense and background (many years' experience between the three).

Abu glanced one final time towards the bow of the boat, over the forecastle and past the bowsprit, across the great expanse of the Marmora Sea and to the Christian boat, which was not much more than a dot on the horizon. He lifted his right hand, which held a baton, and with open mouth gave vocal order at the same time that the baton came down. The beating of the drum commenced immediately, slow at first in order for rhythm to be built, and within the shortest span of time did arrive at a cadence of a mere 15 strokes to every sixty heartbeats.

It was late afternoon on the brigantine, and to the rear of the boat the priests had gathered with Anthony and Toran. It was nothing but the smallest congregation, to put to sea the body of the traitor, who had, after so much pain and torment, given the inquisition the information they desired, although little aid it would bring them.

The two strapping men balanced the foot of the board to rest upon the rear rail, the priests giving final prayer prior to allowing the board to be uplifted, hence delivering its cargo of meat to its final resting place beneath the waves.

The wrapped body bobbed in and out of the water for a few seconds, stabilised, and then sank without further ado, and not a shark in sight. It was then that the group of four looked up and saw the galleass following behind, gaining ground on their brigantine. The oars could be seen quite clearly now, pulling in and out of the Marmora, the sails above billowing in the wind. It was quite inevitable, their capture, the struggle to come. They all doubted that they could win, or for that matter, out run the boat that followed.

Anthony turned his head, he'd heard a sound, and from his peripheral he saw Stephen approach the captain's quarters with Peter in tow. He then looked up to his slight left and right, seeing firsthand the approaching mouth of the Dardanelles, their escape, the only route from Constantinople open to them: mountainous peaks on either side, the mouth of which must have stood at around 18 miles.

"We are entering the Dardanelles now, fathers," announced Anthony.

The first turned and looked for confirmation. "You are too ambitious and optimistic, Anthony. When the strait is but a few miles wide, and only then will we be within the Dardanelles. We will be confined much by restriction in movement. My guess is that we shall be fighting hand-to-hand before first light tomorrow."

"I had heard once," added Toran, "that a boat could gain much speed by posting rowers to the front of their boat, tied fast by a long rope they could pull for more speed."

"It is so typical that such ideas and optimism should proceed ones fear," said the first, looking apologetically at Toran. Here was a man who had fought well and hard during the siege of Constantinople. Such a man as this should not be distressed by the inheritance of an unkind word. He put a palm to his shoulder to comfort the man. "Such harsh words... I am sorry Toran. Regardless of how much additional speed we can muster, we will be caught up with in the end." He removed the comfort of his hand. "Besides, we need to retain our strength for the fight to come. Better to rest and make ready." He looked around at the others, connected with each individual. "Those behind are losing strength, they sap their energy in rowing for speed. We must rest and ensure that we are strong to meet the enemy when they board this boat of ours."

"But the traitor," added Anthony. "He told of over one hundred men, twenty of whom was a detachment of marine."

"Marines won't be rowing," concluded Toran.

The first brought the ceremony to a close: "More the need for rest, for we will have one hell of a fight, once it arrives... and it will come... soon." He walked off with the second priest close behind.

Peter and Stephen stepped from the short fall of rungs and positioned themselves to the front of the captain; he had his back turned on them but soon corrected the rudeness of his stance and faced them both with a smile.

"Captain," said Stephen. "I did hear that the interrogation was complete, and went quite satisfactory... for some."

"If I was a bitter man, Stephen, I would say that you are pinning insult to the back of a dead man; but as I know better, all I can say is yes... and as you have already suggested," Homer sat, "better for some than others." And Stephen could tell that the captain, too, was inflicted badly by the torture. "Better things I have to do than watch over the burning of a man. Not so bad, it would have been, if conducted at the stake, and in earnest. But such are the glories of war, that much torment must be inflicted upon both the enemy and us. But to inflict such terrible wounds to the minds of the innocent, is not a measure I take pride in," and he looked down upon the boards of the cabin in which they stood, indicating the cargo of innocent women and children stationed below.

"Which brings me to my immediate quest," prodded Stephen. "For it would seem that each and every one aboard this grand vessel, has the pumping heart of a professional guardsman, but yet... we lack the weapons." Stephen fidgeted on the spot. "Captain Homer, we have no swords and few spears, the quarrel for crossbow will also be short in supply. If the men and women aboard this boat were Spartans then yes, I could expect them to attack the enemy with tooth and nail, to bite and scratch at the eyes of the enemy, to sink their teeth into the groin of those assaulting them, all in order to draw victory from a one-sided fight. But we have nothing. They know well, captain, to take the sword of a fallen comrade, and how to employ a stick sharpened at one end, in order to tease the enemy with its sharpened point, but tease is all they can do. Surely there must be something... something you have forgotten... some hidden supplies?"

Homer looked upon Peter, hearing all that Stephen had said but refused to answer the question directly, for to do so would only be to agree. It was a common miss conception that people should think he was aware as to what was carried in the hold; for sure, he was captain, but not a cargo master. With the up evils of Constantinople much had happened. Supplies were unloaded, and supplies were secured – many of which was done without his knowing and only hours before the fall of Constantinople was secured. He was Captain Homer: surely these men, aboard this brigantine, had heard of him, and as to how courageously he did fight upon the wall at Seraglio Point. It was then that a little shame befell him, for the fighting he had taken part in was by no means comparably to that of the Mesoteichion: of course he didn't know what was aboard his boat. "Peter, my good fellow, one sworn to the protection of the chest; I need a runner, a good pair of seafaring legs to run my errands and messages." The captain stood and a look of sheer seriousness fell upon him... he thumped the table. "Do you accept?"

"Yes..."

"GOOD! That's all I need to hear, the confidence of a young man as you. Your confidence is brimming, overflowing I say."

"Captain Homer; supplies are in need," prompted Stephen but once again.

Peter looked to Stephen and then back to the captain, Stephen stared Homer down, but only so slightly that no one would have noticed.

"Go Peter. There is no manifest of cargo, no list of provisions that we carry. Go now, Peter, and get me the report that we all wish to hear."

"I shall, captain," replied the youngster. "I shall also make enquires with the sailor, Franco."

"Good man. Feel free to get other to help you if needed."

With that all said and done, Peter did depart the cabin and pushing past the two priests in private conference he went to fulfil his task.

The priests looked at one another, and then to the cabin – something was wrong. And shortly after Peter had disappeared from view the priests crept towards the cabin's entrance.

Peter saw Franco as the group he was lecturing dispersed about, to spend a little more time in familiarity with the boat and its many ropes. Franco sat as though exhausted, letting out a heavy gasp to reflect on his inner feeling.

"Franco," announced Peter as he made his approach. "I have been sent to task by the captain himself, an errand of urgency of which only Stephen can currently concur."

"I would be happy to help where I can, Peter." Franco looked to the rear of the brigantine. "We are short on time, I would guess, so any urgent matter would be best acted upon immediately. What is your urgency?"

"Captain Homer did request a list of provisions."

"Provisions? A list you say? Why, that's absurd, Peter. What time do you have to prepare a list for the good captain, when the damn Turk is clawing at our backs?" Franco contemplated a little. "Do you have quill and ink? NO, don't answer," said Franco, holding up his hand as Peter opened his mouth to reply. "I mean to say: little provision is tucked away, that to find even the most medial of items would be to strain the limitations of our cargo."

"Would you be able to direct me to where my best effort will be rewarded?"

"No, Peter. You will have to look for yourself. Nothing will be found below this deck. Items will be strewn all over. But for food, water is our need… and weapons. Food we can go without, for the fight that comes knocking at our door is but hours away. Weapons dear, Peter, are needed, and they can be anyway… anywhere I say."

"Well, I thank you for your time"

"Wait!" interrupted Franco. "Let me think a minute." The silence lasted but a second; seemed like an eternity. "By God, I have it," and Franco stood, all around turned and gazed. "Lecture adjourned," announced Franco. "Come, Peter. I have something. Quickly, follow me."

Anthony and Toran sat below deck, upon their pallets of blanket and straw. Anthony was sharpening his short sword, as Toran was his single edged broad sword. Toran looked upon Anthony, and in his usual manner gave into wit. "I see you are short on sword, as you are with sense."

"Toran; if you were a stranger to me, I would show you just how short this sword is."

"As short as the one between your legs," a burst of laughter erupted from the mouth of Toran. "You know what they say, don't you? About the size of a man's sword," and laughed some more.

"I should imaging it is the same, that they say about his brains being as thick."

Toran came to his senses then, for the comment hurt. He looked over his weapon of choice, holding it vertical, stroking it gently with a stone he held in the palm of his hand.

"That's why you carry a broad, is it not?" asked Anthony. "For you don't have the brains to influence control over your swords movements."

"Hey; my sword sheers off limbs," Toran hacked at thin air. "What does yours do... scratch the skin, infest with boils the flesh, or brings scars to harbour?"

"She cuts well, Toran; as good as your sword." Anthony punched the air, his weapon an extension of the arm. "I stab and maim, slash and cut, parry and... who is that?" he looked to the entrance of the hold, two men scampering down and disappearing into the shadow at the far end. "Hey! You there! Who is that?"

"Peter," came the answer, the young man answering for himself. "And Franco is with me."

"What are you doing down there, boy."

Franco came out of the shadow and looked the two men over. "I take it that you are talking to Peter? Even so, he is a man, for I heard from several, whom I have but just tutored in the setting of sail that he fought well during the defence of the city."

"Thankyou, Franco," said Peter, "But I need no defence against unkind remarks."

"Unkind remarks," barked Anthony. "I was but teasing. No need to take offence."

Peter shook the remarks from his head; he knew better. "Franco has come to show me something. Quickly, bring a light."

Anthony clambered over the straw bedding and neared the closest lantern within the hold, turning the flame up to better light the area. He walked over the where Franco and Peter stood, Toran content to sharpen his tool of war. "What are you searching for?"

"A barrel," said Franco.

"A barrel of what?" asked Anthony.

"Greek fire."

"Damn!" Anthony nearly dropped the lantern.

"Careful with that light. Treat it like a women… better still, give it to me," said Franco. He took the lantern from Anthony who made protest.

"What for?"

"Because I recall where… ah, ha. Here she is. Just as I thought;" and Franco allowed the light given off from the lantern to bring clarity to that which they looked upon. It was indeed a barrel, with but one marking upon its surface, the mark of skull and crossbones.

Stephen was sat opposite the captain, a tumbler of wine withdrawn from Homer's lips as he swallowed with a resounding gulp. The sea was calm, the temperature outside cool, and the mood of the evening stifling. Homer rubbed at his neck and placed his index fingers into the corners of his eyes, giving them a good rub. He exhaled a breath of defeat, of sheer tiredness, and seemed agitated – if not panicked.

"Stephen, we do not have much time. This boat is small and with many vices running around upon its deck."

"Do you talk of evil, or of people?" asked Stephen.

"Both, my boy… sir knight: oh gentle knight; are you free of the devil… are you pure?" Homer was solemn, meant every word, and spoke as though a poet, and with such soft undertones.

"The devil? No… of course the answer is no."

"The devil exists in everyone, Stephen. All people, even the pope himself has the devil inside. Only the purity of our soles may keep his evil doings at bay." Homer lowered his look, his shoulders falling lax, showing defeat.

"I don't…"

"It is a cancer, Stephen. A plague that inhibits everyone."

"But…"

70

Homer erupted into voice again, looking Stephen in the eye. "I have read the letter that Constantine did give to the priests. In it is much evil."

"But the letter is one of good; is it not?"

"I shall tell you what I remember, Stephen, before we are disturbed." Homer prepared himself for explanation, digging deep into his memory, deciding carefully, but quickly, on how best to describe the contents of the letter. "I cannot recall the exact reading or the quotations where stresses were pressed on particular subjects – although it is all one and the same. The letter from Constantine did announce quite clearly, and without restraint that the contents of the chest should not fall into the hands of the enemy. Most of those that have read the letter believe this to mean those of Islam; but nothing could be further from the truth. We are, all, the enemy, Stephen. Every single person, regardless of his vocation, is the enemy... or rather, has the devil within." His eyes locked well with Stephen's. "This is the enemy, Templar knight. The enemy is the one we have been fighting since the birth of our great salvation; but who is to believe that the fight must begin within; inside us all is where the fight must commence." Homer stood and paced around. "The enemy is not one you can see, but rather feel. His very existence is as real to me as is that tumbler upon my table." He pointed to the drinking vessel and sat down upon his chairs, elbows resting upon the desktop, and he continued with his lecture on the contents of the letter. "It is fair to say that the contents of the chest will empower those of a Muslim faith, by bringing down the Christian." He sat back and waved a hand into the air, brushing away his verbal text as though a crowd of Christian faithful. "Gone forever those of impurity. A Muslim cannot be affected, for his belief belongs to Allah: he has already been recruited by the devil and his worship. The chest holds the scripture of Jesus, a codex of great worth: within the chest is the secret gospel of Jesus... yes, and the look upon your face right now, Stephen, tells of your knowing. I see you believe every word I say, and why shouldn't you? For it is all true. The contents of the chest are true to religion, hidden through the ages to protect the innocent... those that believe they are pure. Anyone holding a supreme position, as that initially heralded as per the Pope, must be free, so wholly, of all corruptness and evil; but this is not always the case. Any amount of activity deemed as inappropriate will see to it that death befalls that individual. Believing in his heart of his honesty, towards the religion and church he has taken to his bosom to embrace, it will all be scrutinized by Jesus himself. Any form of misleading, any swaying from the scriptures, will result in death. No one individual or group must hold the smallest of unfair practise of body or mind. If released, the energy of the chest will strike down any that are impure, and only those with the spirit deserving of sainthood will walk as though free." Homer took a breath, relaxed himself, and then continued. "Eternal life will be given those that are pure, and in order for the word of the Lord to be passed onto the generations, a chosen few, like messengers to travel the passages of time, to pass on the great giving of Jesus and His father, will continue in life on earth, as it is in heaven. A true spirit will be provided for in life. Death of body will not come about, unless someone, or something else, inflicts injury upon it. Even then, only a strike at the heart will render the body lifeless, for other than that, if injury is obtained, then the body will shut down until repaired. It is the heart, Stephen, which holds the gates to heaven, the stairway to everlasting life. It is the heart that is pure, but this can easily become infected by the devil of one's mind. The way in which a person thinks will be is undoing. Anyone can become corrupted of body. The heart Stephen, that is what is sacred." He stood again and turned to look to the galleass – it was gaining on them. "The chest must not fall into the wrong hands, for if the power of the chest is realised, then all those around it will be scrutinized equally. Those of another religion, other than that decree by God, will go unmolested, for the bounds and scripture of their religion will be different, and the guidelines for existence different. Their very belief in the religion of the devil will tax them not." He turned to face Stephen again and sat one final time. "Only once baptised, and surrendered to the life of a Christian, will that individual be swayed by the confines of the chest. All of those of impure body and mind will be struck down without delay. If, however, pure mind and body you keep, as laid down within the scriptures, then you shall reap the reward of eternal life; you will live your life as you deserve, and on death of old age will be given a place in heaven. As for the taking of life," and Homer did stutter a little, slightly confused by what he had read, "this is in fact the surrendering of THAT existence for the one of ETERNAL existence. All of life will be accepted into the realm of heaven, for once death has come to pass we no longer hold power of mind, and the purity of heart takes form. The chest is nothing more than a test, Stephen. If you pass the test then you receive eternal life in heaven, but the selected few will reap the reward and service the Lord for the remainder of time." He scoffed at his own explanation and waved it aside. "HOWEVER, some believe that the contents of the chest, once revealed, will lead to eternal salvation, and that death does not exist for anyone. Of course, the chest must be opened in order for the scripture to be read, but the warning on the chest itself... it must be adhered to. To open the chest in a crowd is dangerous."

Stephen was lost for words. He waited a little, just in case the captain wished to continue, but he was finished with his task for the moment. "If what you tell me is true... then the chest must be hidden away, never to be opened." And Stephen found it hard to believe that Jesus would purposely allow a power to exist that could see to the downfall of His religion. But on the other hand, Jesus was obeying his own scripture, by not preaching prejudicial behaviour – was that correct? "I must also admit that I am wholly confused. Why would Jesus, our saviour, one who did give his life for us, empower the contents of a chest to strike us down like drunken sailors?"

"It is a condition passed down by His father. In order for Jesus to save us from our sins, God did wrought condition. The chest must be opened in order for the scripture to be read," said Homer. "Only then can we be sure."

"And how many times must it be opened? How many times has it been opened already?"

"I cannot answer such questions, and I suspect that the two priests who carry it, will also be unaware of the answer. But I tell you this: I believe in the letter from Constantine, for the bible itself tells of the wrath of God, and of the good of his one and only son."

The door to the cabin burst open and the two priests walked in, careful to close the door behind them. They took their seat in the silence that now dominated the scene. The first looked around the table and spoke with a whisper: "We were outside and heard you talking. Be thankful that no one else was within hearing distance."

"I am surprised you allowed me to finish," said Homer.

"Not only did we arrive late in the discussion, but realised that Stephen is entitled to hear of the letter. Not only this, but to adhere to the scripture of His, I would have to allow you full courtesy and without provocation or rudeness."

"Unless," said Stephen, "we can presume that such rules or guidelines that you preach, dear Father, are of no real meaning or purpose." All looked at the Templar with stabbing eyes. "I listened well to what I was told. I may speak the truth, as I see it, and still be pure of heart."

The second priest smiled. "Stephen, if there is one thing I have learnt over the past few days, it is this: And there shall be no prejudice comparison between servant and master."

"Well spoken," said the first sarcastically. "Is that to mean that Stephen is as holy as the pope and that the pope is nothing more than a lap cat?"

"Not at all, father," replied Stephen. "But it does mean that he is no more pure than I."

"That in itself is the devil talking," accused the first. "For you should not brand yourself of higher station than the representative of our faith."

"Maybe you are right, father; but knowing of the letter and its contents is as important to me as the chests existence is to you."

"I apologise, sir knight, and understand. I understand that you believe you are following the scripture as it is written; even if wrong." The first then turned on the captain. "And what means it that you should believe you have the right to recite the words of Constantine?"

"I thought it helpful… in the current climate. You said yourself that Stephen was entitled."

"So be it," said the first. "It will be the last time in any case." He was then met with stares from Stephen and Homer. "The letter has been destroyed… I… we cannot allow it to fall into the wrong hands, and it would seem we are closer to capture than not," and the look within both priests' eyes gave indication that further was to be said.

Stephen felt as though he saw within the scheme of things, that the priests meant for privacy. He stood up to leave. "I shall be on my—"

"No, Stephen," said the first. "Please stay so that we may talk. There is much we need to discuss in regards to the chest. Please, forgive my rudeness; the good captain is right, all should be revealed to you."

Stephen nodded acceptance and returned to his seat.

The little girl, who had shed a cupful of tears whilst under the instruction of the Teutonic, once again stood to the front of Lars. He was sat upon the deck looking out upon the ocean. There were a few white gulls aloft gliding along on wisps of wind, eyeing the water below for that lustrous feeling of opportunity by finding the catch of the day. He wore a smile that was contagious and slowly it spread to the lips of the girl. She sat beside him and leant her head against his shoulder. She knew what was about to arrive on the galleass that followed, but at this moment felt self-assurance within that all would be okay in the end. They sat there for some time, in the silence; but what conversation could you have with a man who had no tongue?

The girl lifted her head and looked at Lars, who in turn returned the gaze. "My name is Lois," she said. She was of Greek origin (as indicated by the name), most likely born of Constantinople, for no soldier would be docile enough to drag a daughter into the lion's den when hard fighting was known to have been on the horizon.

Lars beamed a smile, so happy to have made a new friend. It did appear that his laying of foundation had won through, and the little girl was no more afraid of him, nor the task to come. And then something shocking did occur, something of which Lars could not comprehend, something that only happened in dreams. Lois looked hard into his eyes and with all seriousness said: "I will kill many men today, Lars; and I will not allow you to be harmed in any way." She hugged the man with all of her strength and rested her head once more upon his strong shoulder, and as eye contact was lost his smile did slowly evaporate, for he had created a beast within this child.

The silence then dominated the surrounds, though Lars' mind was far away. The wind stirred up faint whistling sounds, caused by its current passing over wrought iron and ropes. There was a little cloud in the sky but relatively clear – it was sure to bring on a cold and clear night.

Lars contemplated his past, his time with the Teutonic, the massacre that had taken place during the Battle of Tannenberg in 1410. How lucky he was to have been one of 55 survivors. He considered the death, the blood and the maimed, of how 400 knights were left lying slain upon the battlefield, of how their very dignity had been lost to the enemy. Now it was Lois' turn to meet death face-to-face… if she'd not already done so during the siege of Constantinople. Chances were that she'd been saved from the acts of murder and rape that had taken place, but now it was a different story, she was to become one of the above… murdered or raped. But that was not the end. After rape came death or slavery; slavery, where repeated raping would be the order of the day. She would be better off dead. But she was willing to stand and fight, to see justice rise to the occasion, to put her best foot forward in trying to 'deny' the Turk. It was here, where the Christian forces were to be charged but once again by the devil himself. Here, sometime during the night or early morning, they would once again meet with what they had already met. During the drawing of the curtain in Constantinople a handful of defenders fought against overwhelming odds; those odds were now to be repeated, for the expertise, the very fabric of experience, was all stretched to the limit. At least on the walls of Constantinople they had well-armed, outfitted, and trained men of war, now they had but a handful of experience and cargo load of old men, women, and children. But now this girl, this little child named Lois. She had rekindled something in Lars. Even though he was an experienced soldier, even though he was tough and felt little fear, there had always been something that he had been without, something that he had lost at the battle of Tannenberg in 1410; and that something was about to resurface.

"Lars, Lars, where are you?" said Peter as he saw the knight and the little girl, sitting there in their embrace. "Lars, are you…"

Lars opened his eyes and drew a finger to his lips. The girl, Lois, was asleep, warmed by the flesh of Lars, as though warmed by the comfort of a mother's bosom.

Peter drew closer and knelt beside the knight. "I must ask you to accompany me, Lars. Please come now, for I have something quite urgent to show you, and it cannot wait."

Lars locked eyes with the young man and gave a nod. He would be along shortly.

Peter laid a hand upon Lars' forearm, "Thankyou, Lars," and was gone as quickly as he had arrived. Seconds later and he returned, shrugging his shoulders, opened palm indicating an invitation for Lars to attend, for Peter was expecting the knight to follow as per his request – immediately, and did not understand that the knight meant to attend his urgent need after prying himself gently from the arms of Lois. "Please, Lars. We must go, now."

Stephen wasn't sure exactly what was to be revealed. There was much to the captain's speech that the Templar found disturbing, even though, quite realistically, most of it sounded sane and made sense. But he was delivered a rude awaking, that the idea existed of God's implied conditions; it was simply too much to accept. He had read the Old Testament when he was a young boy and was struck with great awe in regards to the power that God possessed. The New Testament was like the changing of a season, from winter to summer, for the touch of Jesus was so warming and delicate, that the harsh qualities delivered by His father seemed but such a great expanse of difference between the two; or for a single religion to hold so dear.

They all sat and Homer smiled, placing tumblers in front of everyone, including Stephen. "No drink for me, captain, for my wish to remain clear headed is as strong as before."

Homer smiled contentedly and commenced to fill the remaining three cups of wood.

Stephen looked at the captain and considered him carefully. Homer appeared to recite the contents of Constantine's letter so deliberately, even possibly, so accurately, that Stephen questioned it, as to the true merits of the written work, or that it even existed. The fact that two priests had advised of its existence prior to it being destroyed, gave little proof as to its merit and origin.

"Thankyou, captain," said the first.

And further still: if the Emperor of Constantinople was so knowledgeable in regards to the chest, how was it that such information had leaked out or not even employed to aid in the defence of the great city? Was it in fact as Constantine said, and that was that the scripture – whatever it revealed – had no power over the devil, in particular when prevailing within the very structure of another religion or belief. There was also the hint of a miracle, which was to be delivered a chosen one, or few. The only clues he had yet picked up on were that in order to be protected from the confines of the chest, you had to be pure; you could also go unscathed if not yet baptised. But such traits couldn't be right, for how was a new born child, still of crib, to accept baptism with the purity of heart when understanding of such a religion was not yet... wait! That was it: could it be? An understanding of religion must first be attainted before bowing to the codex written by Jesus. What does a small child know except that which it is told? Being forced into religion was like being forced to purity, but purity had to be attained, not forced.

"If this wine is as good as before, I shall be most pleased," said the second.

"It is the same," replied the captain.

Yes indeed: one could not be pure of heart simply because they were being forced. Religion was a structure of learning, a pyramid of steps that lead you to the pinnacle of understanding. Such understanding could not be attained simply because you were exposed to baptism. To first accept baptism, you had to be pure. If baptism was accepted without being pure of heart, then understanding went by the wayside, hence, your ability to mould yourself to the beliefs of the religion you did take to heart, did not actually exist. And then it suddenly struck him... the fact that the devil actually resided within the mind of every man and woman. That was it, surely, the fact that the devil was constantly at play, forcing those of impure heart to accept their chosen belief in God, in order that baptism could be delivered... and on such being accepted, death being embraced.

"There is much being done upon deck; I see Peter running around in great anxiousness," said the first.

"No doubt a boy of heart, but still a man," said the captain.

If the codex of Jesus was as Stephen considered, then many people, if having accepted the word of God through baptism, whilst impure of heart, would be justifiably struck down dead. It was too much to contemplate. It was a test within itself. Only the pure of heart should willingly accept baptism, for to otherwise accept it was to do so under falsehood, and under the very influence of the devil himself.

"But to task we mean to deliberate, and that is the purpose behind our voyage," said the first, putting his tumbler upon the table, the second priest holding his close to his lap, as though in anxious wait.

Homer sat down and looked around, everyone was seated now and locked eyes.

"I am sure there are many questions that dwell upon your tongue, Stephen, like a fire awaiting to be extinguished, or a great thirst looking for that first mouthful of refreshment," said the first. "So few know of the chest, and yet it is a most prized possession." The priest seemed to wonder off, just for a second, as he looked off into the dying night behind the captain, the outline of the galleass standing out quite clearly and just hours away. "Quite astonished I was to hear that Mehmet himself knew of its existence; as though the devil had given the information to him whilst dining in his tent." The priest looked to Stephen and Homer with an apologetic eye. "Understand you both, I should think, as to why it was necessary to destroy the letter?"

Stephen took to answering and in doing so requested further information. "Indeed I do, and quite understandable was your action... but please, can you tell me: what of the chest?"

"Ah, ha; what of the chest indeed, young Templar? What shall be done of the chest and its contents?" The priest's eyelids shot open in emphasis then: "Burn it! No, such a gift cannot be burnt."

"Is this an attempt to ridicule?" asked Stephen.

"Not at all. Please... see it from my point of view. We cannot allow it to fall into the hands of the infidel, any more then we can destroy it. Few options are open to us. We can disguise it as another object; we can open the chest – which would mean defacing it of course – and hiding its contents; or perhaps drop it over the side of the boat."

"To sink and never be found?" asked the captain, a slight chuckle of jest escaping his lips.

"No, of course not. But we could secrete it beneath the boat, where no one is likely to look. But first we would have to ensure the contents would not be damaged; that a clue as to its whereabouts could be left – in case we all die, of course – or that a selected few of us keep such delicate information to themselves."

"And as you have already divulged such information to our ears," concluded Stephen, "we are to be that selected few?"

"Indeed, Stephen, you are," continued the first. "I have deliberated much with my colleague and we have both decided that this is for the best. We would both prefer that it not be necessary, but the galleass, as you can see," he pointed to the boat behind, easily seen through the porthole, "is closing fast."

There was a little silence then as each turned and contemplated the Turk boat, its oars thrashing at the sea, the drumbeat of the coxswain being delivered their ears upon the wind that filled their sails. But much deliberation was still to be met. "So short on time and still the promise you spoke of," all eyes turned to Stephen as he said these words: "that all should be revealed in regards to the chest and the secret it contains."

Anthony, Toran and Franco, stood talking in their leisure as Peter and Lars arrived upon the scene. All were in high spirits, or so it seemed, even though, as Lars looked out upon the rear of the brigantine, the top of the mast belonging to the galleass could be seen quite clearly. They had little more than several hours left and it was growing quite dark.

"Lars, here my man," invited Franco. "I have something which should be of use to you, as discussions with Peter have turned quite ripe."

Lois sat herself against the rail of the boat and remained there in silence as Lars and Peter joined the small group.

Those around continued with small bouts of discussion, bringing to air various points on different subjects. Lars was more interested in what Franco had to say, so concentrate on the subject of his necessity.

"Lars, listen," continued Franco. "We have found this," and slapped a hand upon the barrel of Greek fire. Lars' eyes lit up. "Yes, I knew it. You know well what it is, don't you?" and stabbed a finger in Lars' direction.

And indeed he did. He was quite unfamiliar as to how it ignited, but knew exactly the affect that the substance could have if primed and delivered correctly. "We have many bows and arrows, and this huge barrel of Greek fire. I see no reason why we could not defend our boat now against the infidel. With the bows we can engage the enemy at a distance…"

"As they can us," interrupted Peter.

"Yes, yes; as they can us. But look here; Lars has the good ability to teach," Peter frowned at the suggestion as it was uttered. "Please, Peter; a little enthusiasm if you will." He turned his attention again to Lars. "I am sure that with a little coaching, even with the time we have left, that the men and women aboard this boat can be taught enough to engage the enemy."

Lars was not so sure. It took great strength to pull on the tautness of a strung bow. By the time any structured lesson or familiarity could be taught, they would be too tired to deliver, to the best of their abilities, a well-aimed shot. He looked around and waved a finger. Muffled sound then came from deep within his throat as he first pointed to Anthony, and then to Toran; he gave a nod and then looked around the deck, pointed to Niketas and gave another nod, and then to Rainald, where he shook his head.

"Too old and frail?" questioned Peter.

Lars shook his head and holding up his palms, gave indication that he did not know. Lars then slumped forward as though exhausted.

"Ah, you mean to think that he will be too tired to fight…," said Peter, Lars nodding his head as Peter continued, "after any length of training?"

Franco interceded. "Our strength must not be sapped. We must seek those who hold good hunting ability with bow, even those with little to no ability, but brawn and full of vigour, for they may be able to produce a good shot when the time arrives."

"It would seem to me," said Toran, "that regardless of skill or strength, that when the galleass is within range, we will only be able to get away several shots each prior to us all being stuck like a porcupine ourselves."

"But what choice do we have?" asked Anthony, when the group was suddenly sprung upon by an energetic little girl by the name of Catherine.

All turned their attention to her entrance into the fray of words, as each commenced to bustle for the lectern of place and speech, for each held a different view in respects to how the defence should take form, but the voice of Catherine could be heard to build in volume, to rise above the dying voices of each man: "We could built a raft, a small one, and place the Greek fire upon it."

Peter looked to Lars and then Franco; Franco looked to the decking of the boat and then Toran; and the two mercenaries looked to one another, for they recalled the suggestion made of a rowing boat being placed forward in order to gain an advantage by placing rowers into it.

"Yes indeed!" yelled Toran with excitement. "A raft – or boat – could be placed behind, attached by a rope in order to guide it."

Franco looked to Catherine. "Is that what you wished to convey, young child?"

"It is but one of many ideas, but will give us a slight advantage; I have heard people talking. I have heard of its use before… a story told me when in Constantinople."

"It is a grand idea," insisted Peter, punching his fist into an empty palm.

"It could indeed work," agreed Anthony, "and give us the advantage."

And a muffled sound of agreement came from the tongueless Teutonic.

The messenger landed with a delicate thud, landing flat-footed upon the coxswain's heightened deck, where good visual could be maintained upon the rowers of the mahon. Abu looked to the messenger, Ibrahim, as he appeared at his side, a message from the stern that another vessel had been seen, somewhere to the rear and slightly to the port, closing slowly.

Abu appeared not to be interested, for he knew that any boat or ship that approached from the rear would be none other than a Turk vessel manned ready for war. "A ship or boat, good Ibrahim, and what is the news on its present course?"

"It would appear to be travelling on a course parallel to us, and too far out to currently consider its sovereignty or status. With all that is to be considered, it is best thought to be one of the vessels of our small and weirdly assembled armada," said Ibrahim by his briefest means.

"Very good, Ibrahim. And so I do agree with such an appraisal, for it could be nothing more," and a smile formed upon the face of Abu as he turned to look at Ibrahim. "It is about time that one of our own finally decided to seek us out and bring about a little common sense. The commander of the vessel has done well in deciding to ensure that speed was of the essence. At least now we can rely on a little help... as if we really required it. I think, Ibrahim, that we should reconsider our situation, for it would appear that the boat behind is gaining upon us, which would mean one thing only: it is the mahon of extra sail, for none other could move so swiftly through the sea. Yes indeed, I believe we need to reconsider our situation and reconsider it carefully." Abu looked out upon the bobbing heads of the rowers, the sweat falling from their foreheads, men gasping for air, breathing heavily under the strain of the oars. They were working hard and gaining a good measure of distance on the enemy, the brigantine, and the Christian's hopeless situation.

Abu recommenced to think through his strategy as the messenger Ibrahim turned his attention to the rowers – for a short span of time – before moving off, back to his station at the aftcastle. It would be dark soon, and in the darkness he would find an ally. Abu turned quickly and strode off towards the rear of the boat, to see for himself the vessel that was approaching fast from behind, and as he looked out over the cresting waves of the Marmora he could see for himself that the vessel was indeed a mahon. As he expected it was the boat that held party to extra sail and capable of surrendering rowers for fighting when the need did arise. The best Abu could muster was a top speed and 20 marines; those that followed could slow their advance, though matching his (due to extra sail) and avail themselves to a fighting force of 20 marines and 30 sailors.

How best to tie this to his advantage?

Within minutes he believed, most humbly, that he had the answer. He would ensure that as he closed with the brigantine that he was between the Christian boat and those that followed, in order to deny the information to the commander of the brigantine; and with lanterns drowned he would pass out to a flank, revealing the mahon behind to those that believed in the false god of heaven. The Christians would think nothing of the apparition, rubbing their eyes for confirmation, to see for themselves that, yes, indeed, the mahon behind had slowed in its pursuit and that the gap between them had widened immensely. Why waste his manpower on the fighting to come; better still, if he was quick, and with good measure, he could manoeuvre himself to a position whereby he and this good commander of the other friendly boat could surround the brigantine and board it without so much as a single loss of life.

Abu smiled to himself, a plan that even Mehmet would be pleased to hear. Yes indeed, he was a man of great calibre.

Now what was the commander's name? Think, Abu; you know him by sight.... Abu considered hard all of that which had passed over the days before they had set sail. Ha, ah, he had it. Commander Said. Abu spat contempt, ridding himself of disgusting thought, for he remembered now the hatred and contempt he held for the man. Better Said be burnt in hell than receive favour of pillage and ransom.

The first priest looked into Stephen's eyes and become very solemn. "I cannot... we cannot," he corrected, indicating with a nod, the second, "agree full-heartedly with the letter from Constantine. In it is so much ambiguousness, that it would be correct to point a finger in question. The key to the chest has been locked away in the temple of Káros for many centuries, and the chest itself within the protection of the walls of Constantinople for so long, that it would be far beyond doubt that its contents would have been revealed to the emperor, of past or present. The information within the letter must have been derived from other sources. We believe it's from earlier records, all of that recorded by the founder's mother, Helena. Helena did uncover the sacred artefact of Jesus' burial, an inscription upon a short wooden plank that read: Jesus of Nazareth, King of the Jews."

"But that is not all," interrupted the second.

"Indeed not," continued the first, "for she also came into contact with the chest that we carry, and did ensure its safe keeping by bringing it to Constantinople and delivering the key, in person, to the temple of which we now intend to lay visit. It was recorded by a scribe, that mystical powers were inherent within the chest. Whether such records advised of the chests aspects, or whether Helena was visited by the Holy Spirit, we will never be known... it may even be that Constantine, so recently departed, did receive visions from his mother, or Jesus Himself. One thing we are sure of, however, and that is that the key and chest have not been of the same proximity for over eleven hundred years. This being the case, it is impossible for the letter from Constantine to bear any substantial merit." The priest stopped then, his explanation coming to an end, for there was a build-up of anxious herald coming from upon the deck of the brigantine.

All of those within the cabin immediately looked to the porthole to the rear of the boat, but the galleass was still several hours away. It was then that the cabin door was flung open and in poured, Franco, Lars, Toran, Anthony, and Peter; Catherine could be seen standing in the entrance. Peter looked behind. "Come child, don't wait for an invitation, for it was your idea."

The first priest stood tall and faced the interruption with eyebrows turned inwards. "What is the meaning of this?"

"Forgive us, father," pleaded Toran, "For the child has given us an idea."

"Idea: for what?" asked the first.

"For the defence to come," said Toran.

Peter felt that further information should be posted, and did so diligently. "Your check on provisions, captain, not yet finished, but such a task can wait, for we have found something."

"Several things in fact," voiced, Franco.

"Out with it then, lad," prodded the captain.

"Greek fire, sir, and as much you please, to sink that damn galleass that follows," answered Peter with much swiftness.

"And the girl?" Questioned Homer.

"The idea is hers, captain," continued Peter, "an idea to thwart all others, for we have also found many bows, with a plenty-full supply of arrows. Lars knows," Peter nodded to the man, "that the weapon can deliver a good flame. We set the Greek fire upon a wooden raft, let it out behind and attached to a rope, and when close enough to the front of the galleass we deliver a payload of arrows, each burning with flames good enough to put a finish to those following."

"It will be dark soon, almost upon us already is the night," said Toran. "It is our only chance to impede the enemy in order for us to make good our escape into the Aegean."

"We may even sink her," concluded Franco.

The priests looked to the captain, the importance of their explanation in regards to the chest well and truly forgotten.

"It may well work," said the first.

"Sounds sweet to the ear," said the second.

"A grand idea," said the captain. "Franco, set upon preparation; take some men and ready a raft. Toran and Anthony, bring forth the Greek fire. Lars, prepare your bowmen – and women." Homer stood, continuing with orders. "Stephen, get ready your men for battle, and fathers, pick your ground well, for once the Greek fire is ignited there will be little place to hide, for the night will be as bright as the day."

They had been waiting half the night, but finally they could hear the galleass, the coxswains drum, the oars thrashing at the sea, and then suddenly, appearing out of the night, a silhouette did appear. Most of the lanterns upon the enemy boat had been extinguished, though surprise was never to be gained, for those of the brigantine had known of their intended capture to come. They were reliant upon the wind alone, where the enemy were able to draw upon sail and the stroking of the sea; the noise was enough to awaken the dead, let alone scare them out of their skins. Certainly, not, no surprise at all, and the enemy would too be aware of the Christians lying in wait.

But they had a little defensive strategy. The brigantine had allowed a single lantern to remain alight, enough to give signal to the galleass that followed, that they were indeed still being gained upon, to lead the hunter into a false sense of security; they also weakened one of their own sails, so that when the need arose they could be granted more speed.

All was quiet upon the deck, men and women ready for a quick fight and easy escape. All they needed to do was cripple the galleass enough to allow them easy passage to the mouth of the Aegean, and the rest would be history. The captain, for one, didn't wish to make an artificial reef of his boat, any more than he wanted the flesh of his body to be food for the sharks.

Stephen had a few men ready with sword, hiding behind the rail of the brigantine, and in front of the cabin – though little protection that would be from a straight-flying arrow. Niketas and Rainald were to his left and Catherine to his right, spear in hand. There was also Lois, a child with crossbow at the ready, prepared to shoot at any man trying to board their boat, as well as two other girls of similar age, Zoë and Irene, both holding tight to short swords and several quarrels.

Further to the forecastle of the brigantine, ready to move towards the stern, forward into firing position beneath the mainsail, were six men of their later years, 5 women, several boys and Peter. Toran and Anthony were at the side of the boat, having lowered the raft and its cargo into position – they held tight to the rope, ready to feed this through their palms when the time was right. The captain maintained vigil upon his crew and cargo in order to ensure the defence held strong: he personally was to ensure the brigantine was steered slightly to the port in order to allow the raft easy movement in its short journey to the front of the galleass and hence securing them their victory.

Toran and Anthony had attended their task with great anticipation, having lashed the barrel of Greek fire to the makeshift raft of planks and posts. The lid of the barrel had been damaged slightly in order to allow the combustible to be easily lit, having been spilt enough to cover the wooden raft, soaked well with the contents of mixture. All that was needed was for a single arrow to hit the raft and the night air would be filled with a great calamity of noise, burning flame, and volumes of black smoke.

The two priests had given to prayer, but had also taken position within the cabin, to avail themselves a little cover as they set upon delivering a few well aimed crossbow quarrels to the galleass that followed, and it would not be long now before it was upon them. They had also decided against surrendering the chest to station below the waves, for the priests were optimistic and couldn't bear to see the chest ruined or lost for ever.

Lars crept forward to a position just behind Stephen with crossbow at the ready, having just seen to the late delivery of Franco, Master Andrew and John, to the two priests below. Other less endowed women and children were spread out upon the deck, ready with spears and sword, prepared to throw these aside to help with the rigging and tacking of the brigantine when the time did arrive, as well as being able to attend to the wounded. Sailors aloft had also taken to the deck, ready with sword for killing and able hand for the setting and shifting of sail.

The orders of the boat's commander could be heard above the beat of the coxswain's drum, the oars churning up the water loaning fear to all, a dragon's breath and heartbeat allowing panic to mount; and the priests eyes bulged with fear as the sail and bow of the galleass came into view, to be plainly seen to be decreasing the gap between the two, both Muslim and Christian drawing closer, the gap between the two closing quickly. The galleass, its bow pulling up out of the water, surging forwards with each stroke of the oars, seemingly preparing to ram the brigantine, and with this thought entering the minds of those that witnessed the galleass gain ground came a sobering thought: in order for the enemy to draw upon so much speed, must mean that very few of the enemy were ready with weapons that could strike at a distance. This was news to be taken to the heart, a cherished moment which would be short lived, for if the Greek fire failed, and the initial flurry of arrows were wasted upon the raft and sea around, then they were in for a hard fight of hand-to-hand – the barrel of combustible upon raft must be a success, for anything else spelt the end of their voyage to safe harbour.

Homer then gave a whispered command for the brigantine to change direction and the raft loaded with Greek fire was allowed to float away towards its target, the coarse rope being fed through the hands of Toran and Anthony. All appeared well, the raft was on target, and the galleass seemed to gain in speed – although the beat of the coxswain's drum didn't change and nor did it miss a single beat.

The time was almost upon them and then suddenly on command, from the hold, did appear several young boys with torches alight, to set flame upon the arrows that were cocked and ready to be released into the cold night air. And as each arrow was ignited into flame, each was released into flight, streaking through the breeze, from point 'A' to point 'B', the shallow trajectories of each shot being visible to anyone looking into the night, where not even the moon gave aid, for it was still below the horizon; and with the mystical sight of fire in the air came a muffled scream from the galleass, and the coxswain's drum thundered into a rhythmic sprint, the boat behind surging even further out of the water then it had before.

Shudders of fear shot through the Christian crew and gathering of passengers, seeing first hand that the arrows were falling into the sea around the raft, missing the target completely – and this be a lesson to the Christians, for as they watched, they were neglecting their responsibility, for no more arrows had been strung in readiness to deliver a follow-up of the preparatory.

Peter looked to his side and spat out the command, rushing up and down the line, pushing them forward, and ordering for better fire positions to be taken. The bows had to be employed, a continuous rain of arrows had to be maintained, and the Greek fire had to be ignited. It was then that the true horrors of war commenced to take its toll, for out of the darkness came the whistling of air rushing past shaft, for the infidel had let loose with their own shower of pain and death, arrows appearing out of the night, streaking towards their targets as though lead to them, like rain delivered from a thunderstorm, though alone a horizontal plane, and as the old men and women fell in screams of pain and torment the galleass struck hard against the brigantine. Suddenly a heathen crack could be heard by all around, for something had bore the brunt of the ramming and would take its toll on the seafaring ability of the boat and its refugees... if they should live.

People fell to the deck and quickly stood again, one old women remaining their on her side, clenching at her leg, for it had been broken below the knee, the bone protruding the flesh of her leg, a dribble of blood seeping to the cold night air. And too, the blood of the dead and dying commenced to flow, seeping into the cracks of the timber, and running here and there towards the rail of the brigantine.

Toran and Anthony held onto the rope as best they could. Their initial target was to be the front end of the galleass, but they could not control the raft any more than the tide of the waters around. The raft drifted slowly but surely, along the port side of the boat of the enemy. It was hard to see as it bobbed up and down with the waves of the sea. It was sure to be a hard target to hit, even with the little illumination about to be given off by the arrows in the air and the few lanterns aboard the brigantine.

Stephen could see well all that was being delivered by the Muslim men aboard the galleass, yet he was in no position to do anything except wait. His hand shot up and pulled the head of Catherine down behind cover, offering his body as protection, as best he could. An arrow then hit hard against Zoë's chest, forcing a last gasp of air out of her lungs, death being delivered unto her as quickly as life had been accepted on birth. Irene then stood in panic, an arrow hitting her square in the face.

Peter turned in horror, looking down upon the deck, his eyes shooting a glance upon the bodies of two boys, two of the three who had put flame to arrow. "Draw your bows! Fire when ready! Don't wait for the command! Boy, BOY; THE FLAME, BOY, GET THE FLAME!"

The child was alone, standing there in shock, his friends dead, with arrows sticking out of their back. He clamped his jaw shut then and pulled himself together, shaking the grief from his mind, setting light to arrows as they were pulled to the ready by the women standing their ground.

A woman of old age saw the calamity, fell to her aching knees, snatched a torch from the clenched fist of one of the dead boys, the other beside him, gasping for air – he was still alive – for the arrow had pierced his lung. He was drowning in his own blood. The woman stood and put flame to more arrows as several of the younger women drew on their bows.

The arrows flew through the air, passing in mid-flight another flurry from the galleass, enemy arrows which were ten times in number compared to those fired by the Christians, Muslims in their dozens standing upon the fore and aftcastle. More women took the brunt of the wall of iron as it struck hard the Christian defence and the decking, Peter, too, receiving a shot to the head. The last of the boys then whirled around, pivoting on the spot, seeing a lone man of wrinkled flesh standing as crooked as could be, holding tight to a strung bow, awaiting to be kindled with flame. The boy went to him, fast upon his feet, and as the flame was delivered its arrow, the boy fell heavily to the deck, an arrow having pierced his neck, cutting the main artery between head and shoulders.

The arrow was let loose, spent of the bow, reaching its halfway point unobstructed by mast, sail, or body of flesh, and then commenced the final leg of its journey, striking the barrel mid-on. The Greek fire exploded then, a ball of flame leaping into the air, illuminating both boats in their entirety. Men, women, and children dropped their weapons of war to shield their eyes from the burning brightness, and as quickly as all was lit, so it died in the wake of the fire it had born, to become a burning furnace of flame. The front side of the galleass nearest the brigantine was burning feverishly, and amongst the mayhem came the screams of several Turks, heard to mingle with the sounds of war as a command to board the Christian boat with scimitars drawn came to the ears of Stephen and his good friend Lars.

Along the port side of the galleass, oars were being pulled to boat and those that burnt were flung to the sea. The vessel was turning to meet the flank of the brigantine, the ramming of one vessel against the other having the effect of forcing the two together, like the hinge of a great wooden door helping to draw one plank to another. And for a short second a little joy did leap into Homer's heart, for he could see what had made that heinous sound of cracking wood: the short bowsprit of the galleass had snapped in half and its foremast had buckled – though such a small mast it was, and of little consequence. And as his mouth opened with a smile an infidel's arrow did strike and pierce the back end of his throat – death being instantaneous.

The flame along the side of the galleass commenced to spread. Several Christian sailors saw the closing threat and took action to ensure that extra speed was attained, and by tightening the sail and pulling in unison the ropes around, the brigantine leapt forward as though refreshed after a long race. Several men cheered then, though drowned by the fire that fed off the galleass; but the fight was far from over.

The bow of the enemy boat, although damaged, was still close enough to the brigantine for men to take a run and leap. Half of the contingent of marines made it across, several falling into the sea, its surface burning, coated well by Greek fire. Some had their scimitars at the ready when they made the jump from boat to boat, others sheath their weapon of choice to be revealed once safely upon the Christian deck. It was now that the hand-to-hand commenced to play its role in the fight for survival, a survival that the passengers and crew had been fighting since well before their escape from the Golden Horn of Constantinople.

It was no surprise to see that Stephen was the first to meet the assailants, taking two angry men on, putting in a well planted parry, followed immediately by a downward slash across the infidels' legs. Screams erupted from the Turk, and before any man or woman could blink an eye – or believe what they were being told was witnessed: unless, of course, seen for themselves – Catherine did charge in with her spear, thrusting it hard into the belly of the second. The contortion on the Turks face spoke its own meaning, for his eyes locked with the child. So close he did come to slicing off the face of Stephen that the joy of the soon-to-be victory had commenced to grow within him; now all he had was the penetrating point of a spear sticking in his gut, held by the hand of a six year old girl. A snarl then formed upon Catherine's face and she yanked the spear free, immediately crouching down behind the Templar, awaiting the opportunity for her next victory.

Lars was crouched upon one knee and spent a quarrel. He released his grip to grab another and became startled, faltering for a second to collect the true nature of what was occurring, for Lois had placed into his palm a missile, its point facing forward, ready to be loaded and fired. And Lars did not disappoint, for no sooner had the quarrel been placed within his hand he did fire into the small crowd of marines as they boarded the brigantine.

The quarrel was fast and flat, burying itself deep into the belly of a man as he landed sure-footed upon the deck, and as Lars looked up and readied to replenish his crossbow but once again both Anthony and Toran leapt past him, joining in on the melee, not wishing in a hundred years to miss out on the fight.

Niketas and Rainald sat cowering just behind the group now in melee, when they saw how Catherine had delivered her thrusting spear, and to how the two mercenaries had leapt without second thought into the building fray they lost all conviction. They looked at one another. How could they sit back like this, hiding from the fight, as though clawing for protection? Was it not bad enough that they both turned down the opportunity to fire the bow, in pretence of favouring to fight with the sword? How many women and children had lost their lives already? Enough was enough, for no man could live with himself under such pressing circumstances. They drew their swords then and stood up with their conviction restored, Rainald immediately being delivered his place in heaven for an arrow pierced his heart. The sheer anger that welled within Niketas could have been likened to the build-up of pressure within the depths of the earth itself, prior to the rupture of a volcano, it letting loose its destruction of rock and fire. A yell so terrifying came from deep inside of him and with sword held high he joined in on the fight for survival, for if a six year old had the courage to protect him from harm, surely he could do the same in return.

The clash of sword upon sword, and scream of encouragement mixed with scream of death and terror, was all too much to bear for those few that were hidden within the cabin of the brigantine.

95

The priests knew not how to fight or steer a boat; fire a crossbow, maybe: they knew only of prayer and psalm, of preaching and service, of burial and of how to forgive those that sinned. The two boys with them were not much better off; what did they know of fighting. But if they could have seen the fight that Catherine and Lois did deliver to those that called themselves the righteous and only religion, of how they spent their sweat and good nature to help win the fight, then they would not have been hiding. And as the fighting above them grew in ferocity so did the torment within their hearts… and one final note struck them hard, for they suddenly heard Catherine screaming at the top of her lungs, for she had delivered another thrust with her spear, bringing down another of the marines who had boarded their boat.

Franco looked at the two boys, grabbing them by the shoulders. "The time has arrived men," and the eyes of the children grew wide with hunger on hearing Franco speak that word: men. "The time has arrived. The fight will not come to us; we must go to it. Come! COME I SAY; let us skewer those infidel like there is no tomorrow." And as he drew his sword from within his scabbard of wood, the boys, Andrew and John, picked up the short swords that had been handed them by Lars prior to his earlier departure. Franco looked to the door of the cabin, the corner of his mouth pulling up, anger so fierce being portrayed as the main feature of his face. A scream then erupted and he raced into the night, to find himself a victim, to kill himself a heathen Turk, for no devil-maker deserved to stand upon the deck of a Christian boat, in particular one on which he had sailed for so long. The boys followed suit, yelling, as did Franco, joining in on the fight above them, to partake of the horror that had been dealt them, to do what they could in the name of the Lord.

The melee continued to be as vicious as it was, but no sooner had Franco and the two boys turned out to meet the foe which awaited them and the sail pulled taught so well it did harness the wind as expected and commenced to pull the brigantine away from the danger. The gap between galleass and brigantine grew, as did the fire upon the hull of the enemy's boat. The flame licked up the sides, spreading left and right. A little cloth caught alight and this sparked embers that lifted with the heat from the fire as it burned, delivering them to the dry sails above. Within minutes the entire boat of oarsmen had proceeded to douse the fire as best as possible, making easy targets for Lars' crossbow as they dipped their buckets and other paraphernalia into the sea for water to smother and put out the death that currently enveloped them. And Catherine, as sweet and innocent as she was, partook in the killing, drawing up alongside Lars and commenced the shoot quarrel after quarrel into the mass of men as they attempted the impossible.

Few of the enemy were left alive upon the deck of the Christian boat, so few indeed that Andrew was the only one of the three latecomers to have a jab at the stomach of an infidel as the body fell backwards from wounds delivered by Stephen's sword. It was then that shouts for all to take cover were received by all ears, for the enemy knew they had lost the day and were now making a handful more pay the price for the victory won, by letting fly with more arrows, several of which had been soaked in fat and were burning as brightly as the boat left in the wake of their glorious escape. Several more women and old men, along with the child, John, met with death. Franco was the last to die that night, as he, holding onto the brigantines mainmast, leant out to yell obscenity to the infidel as they slowly sank.

And the boat proceeded into the night, along the narrow strait of the Dardanelles, further and further from the sea that burned with fire, and the last glimpse of the wooden galleass disappeared from view forever as it sank beneath the surface of the waters around.

By mornings first light several dozen bodies had been delivered unto the sea, the priests having paid special tribute to the slain, for they had given their lives so that others may go on in life. Old men, and in particular, women, too frail to tend themselves, by all realistic measure, but they had put forward a stiff upper lip to deny the devil his victory.

The sun commenced to bring light to day and with it the four remaining sailors – after the carnage – took to evaluating the true condition of the brigantine, Andrew following in their footsteps, learning all he could in regards to the seamanship that was being displayed before him. He felt a heavy heart for the loss of Franco, but so did others aboard the boat, in particular his drinking mates of sea and ocean. The world they had seen, and a little more too; voyages into the far horizon that had brought them all many adventures and sore heads. Arguments between friends often broke out where women were concerned, a lovely lass her, one there; wherever the tide decided to take them they would leave their heart... and the contents of their purse, for their thirst for women was as strong as it was for wine.

There was an old man below deck, holding onto dear life, and not through careless action, or mortal injury to flesh or bone. His actions of the night before were as heroic as they could be, but his age: too old in flesh for rescuing damsels in distress, let alone a boat full of aging men, women and children. He was seen to fight as the others, where he could... and it was he, who had set light to the Greek fire. He was to be congratulated, to be given a good slap on the back for a job well done, but alas, he was too frail for such compliment and remained upon his pellet of straw and blanket being attended to by Niketas.

Lars was also resting below deck, worn out from the scuffle, the melee that had come to hand. His palms were red raw from pulling on the poundage of the stock of his crossbow, and his sword bloodied from point to sword hilt. He wore the brunt of several cuts to the face and lower arms, where his chest plate did nothing to protect – if anything the armour proved to be little more than an inconvenience; he should have known better and have removed the plate prior to engaging in close quarter action with the enemy: for compared to him they were weak in mind and spirit. Yes indeed, he had committed himself, and fought like ten men, so proud were others to be associated with the knight of old. Lois was with him now, and as tired as she was she simply adorned the man who was once a Teutonic. As he slept she bathed his face in a little warm water, a commodity that had been surrendered to her by one of the sailors above.

Anthony and Toran had committed themselves to other duties, such as tending the women who had survived the fight – there were only four of them now, and one of those had a badly broken leg. They had heard Stephen put mention to the injury earlier on, that the leg would most likely have to be removed in order to save her life. Short argument did arise in regards to this, for all were aware that they were heading for Káros, where there was an abundance of Hospitaller knight, all quite capable of performing their charitable work and surgery upon her leg.

Catherine stood by Stephen, even now. They were both steady as a rock, standing upon the decking of the forecastle, looking out past the bowsprit as it moved gently up and down in respect to the scene of the sea beyond it. The sea was comparatively calm. It was a cloudless day, a light breeze blowing from the rear, and there was no sign of an enemy vessel, until....

"Full to the bow: galleass for sure!" yelled the sailor from the perch of his station upon the mainmast. "She looks to be blockading our escape into the Aegean. I see the mouth of the Dardanelles to my front. The boat is steady in the water, not a sail to be seen."

Stephen – looked to by many to now be in command: without anyone actually committing to such a comment – glanced up to the sailor. "How far?"

"Could be two leagues, possibly three... at the most," spat the sailor as he remained at station. "Nothing from the port nor starboard, all clear to the stern."

"How long have you been aloft?"

"Just this minute, Stephen," the sailor a little confused at the question, looking down to the man he had relieved.

Stephen then looked towards the main cabin of the brigantine, a sailor slipping into it as though trying to go unnoticed, the man who had just left his post and lookout.

Stephen's softened look peered down to the face of the child at his side. She was steadfast, no hint of discouragement, no ounce of fear. Catherine was cast of iron, an unbreakable link in the chain that the survivors now formed. He turned on his heel: "I must speak with the priests."

Ibrahim attended his orders as good as good can be, slipping quietly into Abu's quarters with not so much as a sound. The only reason Abu knew of his entrance was to the fact that he was facing the door to his cabin. He looked up from the chart sprawled upon the table. "What do you have, Ibrahim?"

"The brigantine is heading this way. No sign of any other boat. At least two leagues out at present, and heading directly towards us. I should think that they are aware of our being here."

"What makes you say that, Ibrahim?"

"A guess, Abu. Nothing more."

"Guesses can be fatal, Ibrahim; very fatal: but naturally they see us." The captain looked down to his chart, pointing a finger. "It is well that we left the brigantine to that dog of a captain, Said, that was following in our wake. I hated the man, to tell the truth." He looked Ibrahim in the eye. "It was due to him that I fell out of favour with the admiral. But things will change soon. The Christians may have gotten away clean... lucky for them – and us – that they had the Greek fire, employed well I must say and easy to see as it burnt the night sky so brightly. I doubt very much that they have anything of substantial value left in their boats hold that will serve them well in any further defence. Only cunning will tell the story, Ibrahim, and I believe we have that right here. Our

100

munitions are as they were when we departed Constantinople; our rations are as they should be and no one thirsts for fresh water. We can stay here; right where we are, for several months and a few days more, if we have to. By then a friend is sure to drop by, prodding that scum of a Christian boat right into my hand. No, they won't wait around. It shan't be long and we will have our catch. They have no choice but to attack in order to make it into open water; if they do that, they've defeated us, but I shan't allow that to happen. Like thieves in the night we stole this victory. Redeployment has worked its miracle. We will have our catch of the day, and soon."

"Ah, good Stephen, sir knight," said the first as the man of youth and charisma clambered down into the confines of the cabin. "We were just speaking of you, concerned we are in regards to what actions you tend to sally from our little victory."

"Rations we need," added the second.

Stephen turned to Catherine, who followed. "To the entrance, I wish not to be interrupted."

Catherine gave a nod of her head, accepting the order (which came sweet and so softly, as to be a request) and departed. The sailor present sat down next to the first.

"I wish to know your names, and if I do not receive them, here and now, I swear to you both that you will be dispatched ashore this very moment, and without your chest of secrets," commanded Stephen, looking down at the sailor who was previously aloft and then both of the seated men of God, their robes stained from weeks of wear, only their hands and heads revealed to the world. They were a poor sight, patches of discoloured cloth sewed into place where the fabric had warn thin, holes having once appeared where the squares of material had been placed. Stephen was

101

particularly drawn to the large stain that was evident at the waist of the first, a thick stain of oil that was easily seen, and not present on the previous day of the voyage, when the knight had last laid eyes upon them.

The first looked to the second, the other did the same. The first spoke: "If I am not mistaken, I should think that you are giving us an ultimatum."

"You may take it as you wish, I care not," Said Stephen, and sat upon a chair. "All I care about now is for the safety of those aboard."

"Then to waste time taking us ashore would—"

"Who said anything about taking you ashore," Stephen faced the first in reply. "I mean only to advise that you shall be dispatched; it would be stupid of me to think that you would wish to reside upon the waters of the Dardanelles to rot upon a raft, in particular with the enemy not so far away. Does torture ring a bell?"

"The heathen Turk, torture… I would prefer to drown than…"

"STOP THIS, DAMN YOU!" Stephen thumped the tabletop so fiercely with his clenched fist that one of the tumblers of wine upon the table went sprawling, its contents drifting to the edge and depositing the wine upon the robe of the first.

He stood in a huff. "You clumsy fool!"

Stephen drew the sword, quick as quick can be, and its point just inches from the chin of the man in robes.

"Sit," said Stephen calmly, "you damn Turk."

"What is the meaning of this?" stammered the second. "What are you saying? Have you lost your mind?"

"I wish it was as simple as that," continued Stephen. "You see, the good captain Homer did speak to me prior to us having taken station last night; before the fight."

"Ah," was all that the first could register. "And you think that he spoke the truth?"

"I have not yet revealed what it was that Homer was supposedly to have said, yet you seem confident in the knowledge that something indeed was spoken in ill-will." Stephen paused. "Can you explain this?"

"This is absurd!" shouted the second.

"Not at all, father, for I do not speak of the Turk torturing you, but of the torture you did carry out upon the traitor," said Stephen calmly.

"I see not…" started the second, but the first held up his hand.

"It is alright, brother. Please abstain from my defence. The Templar has the right," no longer a friend, it would seem, by the way in which the first did address, Stephen. "Please, tell me what you know and you shall be granted the truth."

Stephen had made a little ground, but nervous all the same… and the sailor who sat in silence; he was the one… he was the other traitor.

Catherine had been stationed and stood her ground. She had been set to task and was committed to the order given by the Templar. Her stomach then grumbled, hungry for something to eat. She licked her lips – she needed a good drink too.

She saw a few gulls flying through the air, a little cloud here and there. She commenced to daydream then, when one of the others onboard approached her with a smile upon his face.

"Good child, what are you doing standing here?" asked Niketas.

"I am on guard… at the request of Stephen," answered Catherine.

"Why, child? What is going on inside that chamber of misery?"

"Misery?"

"It's a torture chamber, child. It is where brave men are tortured for the truth."

Catherine could see the devil surfacing in the eyes of the man named Niketas, and she didn't like it. "You are scaring me. I wish you to stop."

"Ah," said Niketas, bursting into a smile and giving Catherine's head a good rub. "I'm only teasing you, Catherine. But tell me, before I enter, what is being said."

"I do not eavesdrop, not for nobody. It's rude and insulting."

Niketas stood tall, tired of the game. "Come child let me past."

"No, you cannot enter, I have my orders."

"Are you a girl or a soldier? Let me past before I lose my patients with you." He looked down upon Catherine: she was stubborn and intolerable. He then gave plain notice that intimidation and access was his desire. "NOW, CHILD!"

"Captain Homer did advise me that during the act of torturing the traitor, you, father," Stephen indicated the first, "did request that your brother of the cloth did attend some urgent need. The need is not important, for the good captain was so sickened by the torture, that most of what was said could not be recalled by him. But such is the ploy you performed in ensuring that no other, familiar with the rudiments of torture, were present. It was then that I decided to commence my private investigation and to put together my thoughts."

"Please," said the first, arms now crossed, "continue."

"Toran and Anthony are mercenary, not conversant with methods employed by an inquisition. It was you, father, who suggested the captain employ their services. Not only this but you were also seen to be conversing with the traitor... how should I say: quite secretively. You were quite ready to dispose of your accomplice priest, during the torture, when it suited you best. There was also the lantern that was employed by the traitor to signal the galleass behind. It took me awhile to realise, and in all honestly, shrugged from thought… but it is yours, father. I saw it sitting beside your sleeping pallet."

The second priest couldn't believe what he was hearing; he was utterly dumbfounded. The first then ushered the Templar to continue with his speech. "Please, something else perhaps?"

"Oh, yes indeed, father. You were quite aware of your Brother's warming to torture," and Stephen indicated the second. "Giving the traitor a warning – and possibly even indirectly; how else was he to know of the impending pain to come?" Stephen gave way to another pause, as short as his first, looking around briefly to ensure all were attentive. "You had few instruments of torture prepared, indicating to me that you were in fact after a quick end to the traitor's life, as opposed to what should really have been the appropriate measure of a long and hard format of question and answer – I was surprised your brother didn't pick up on this, and nor did he say anything."

"Are you accusing me of being an accomplice to your false accusations?" questioned the second with an air of fright.

"Not at all, father, but please, let me continue. I can also tell you that the stain upon your robe is in fact from the same oil that was present upon the feet of the traitor. You were quite discreet when removing a large quantity in order to relieve the traitor of his torment, by rubbing your robe against his feet. The traitor was even polite enough to call you, father: during torture… absurd. Yes indeed, I have asked questions of Toran and Anthony, enough to convict; but let me finish. From what I can understand, it was shortly after the traitor was questioned in regards to, 'who else amongst us preaches as you do?' that your brother was sent on errand." Stephen let out a little exhale, as though slightly satisfied. "And, of course, you, father," again Stephen indicated the first, "kept your promise and gave the traitor a drink of water; one that had been spiked with poison."

"Are you finished?" asked the first.

"All except one task," and with that said the Templar thrust out with his sword, like a strike of lightening, penetrating the heart of the sailor who sat at the table, the sailor who had clearly seen the enemy waiting but had not reported it. A horrible contortion to the facial features presented itself; the priests were sickened – even if strong – and the hands of the sailor, having gone to the aid of the injury fell limp. "For the reason the traitor was able to send a signal to his rear was because the man at the helm at the time was none other than this dead man before me," and withdraw his sword from the scabbard of flesh, blood momentarily squirting out upon the table surface before flooding copiously over the sailors dirtied silk shirt.

"NOW, CHILD!"

"What…" Stephen stepped back carefully from the table, the body of the sailor slumped over, dead.

Niketas pushed the child aside with gusto, Catherine falling to the deck, but soon back upon her feet. The cabin door burst open.

"What, in the name of God, is going on?" asked Stephen, shocked at the intrusion.

"I would like to know the same," and Niketas saw the body of the slain. "My God." He rushed forward.

Stephen looked past Niketas as he rushed past, seeing that Catherine was alright: "I am sorry, Stephen."

"It is alright." Stephen felt for the child. "Please, Catherine, you have done nothing wrong; go and see to your nourishment."

"What has happened here?" Both priests were standing now, as calm as calm can be. "This man is dead," stated Niketas, for he was confused enough to think that the obvious had eluded those present. "What is the meaning of this?"

"He was a traitor, Niketas," explained Stephen. "He was an accomplice to those who have been sent to see to our demise."

"My God… how many others can there be?"

"Just one, Niketas," said Stephen. "Only one other traitor exists amongst us." He looked to the first priest and back again. "And what is your urgent need, Niketas?"

"The old man is dead, but his legacy shall live on."

"We know not of your previous vocation, but to the fact that you are born of the devil, we must cast you aside," said Stephen.

The remainder of those aboard the brigantine had gathered around; others that could not be taken from their errands, tasks, or commitments, were elsewhere. The first priest looked up from the makeshift raft, where he had been deposited. He was lucky to still be alive, but as Stephen had said, enough blood had been spilt, and the spilling of one more would not make an overall difference. The first priest and those in the galleass that pursued them already knew about the chest, so the priest's death would not achieve anything; the priest was sure to be rescued of his predicament and in some small part might be reprimanded for his failure. The chest was now stored below deck, in safekeeping, to be delivered the temple in Káros. There was at least two to three galleass behind them and one more up ahead. No other words of farewell were given, no calling of indictment considered. And as the priest pushed away from the brigantine in silence, Stephen turned to the other and addressed him, as he should. "Father Norotus. The old man from the night before, the brave sole he keeps; he must be released of his worldly sins and bitterness, given a place in heaven, for his actions did speak louder than words, and the devil he does not possess. He is as pure as they come."

"Indeed, Stephen," agreed Norotus, the priest who now considered that he had a flock, and such a flock must be tended to. He shook Stephen's hand and smiled. "You are in command of us all, we all look to you as our saviour, and I hope in all sincerity, that you have a plan for us to employ. For the Turk sits in our path and it would seem, there is no way out, but straight ahead."

Norotus attended his flock and Stephen considered the idea behind the priests' names being kept secret: it was simply a measure of security, which the first had put into place to ensure his identity remained unchallenged. But now, with structure and commitment being laid, all of those upon the brigantine knew his and her place. As the gathering dispersed, Stephen saw one final act that brought comfort to heart. Niketas was down on his knees, looking Catherine square in the eye, giving his most humble of apologies, for his rude, and unforgivable actions and remarks.

All aboard the brigantine knew of the galleass, sitting in wait as it was; what they didn't know was of the sails tied away neatly, prepared with slip knots to be unfurled with the quickest of ease, oarsmen at rest, marines preparing their weapons for battle, and the commanders lying back in their pallets of blanket. But it was an educated guess that an enemy, in particular, one in full view, would take advantage of every minute that passed them by. The distance between the two vessels was a little over one league, and with the current speed and tacking of sail, the two weren't presumed to clash any time early: but most assuredly before mid-afternoon. There wasn't much chance of slowing the advance any further, without actually going backwards, and to go back, into the advancing hand of three enemy boats, was not as favourable as continuing on course for the Aegean, where only one enemy galleass was currently at station.

Stephen had called for a general meeting of all of the survivors, of which there was only fifteen (sixteen including himself); this list of fighters consisted of the following: Lars, Lois, Andrew, Niketas, Catherine, Anthony, Toran, Norotus, three sailors [Fabian, Eben, Jacob] and four women [Lucia, Dorothea, Eve, Drusilla]. The woman, who had approached Stephen the night before, offering her assistance in regards to nursing, had not survived the fight, and little need for such services existed at present in any case – apart from the woman with the broken leg, and that needed more than the gentle touch of a nurse. Introductions amongst the crew and passengers were made and predicament indicated quite strongly. When the time came to fight they would all have to do their part in bringing down the enemy attack: although, as Stephen saw it, attack was the best defence in some cases, their predicament being such a scenario. The wounded and dying would have to fend for themselves until such a time that the brigantine was well clear of the enemy boat – that was surmising that they could in fact escape the Turks' clutches. Once escape had been secured, and a course set and sails full of wind, they would be able to breath a little easier and attend to anyone with a wound: until such a time, however, it was every man, woman, and child, for themself.

"We shall have to take the fight to the Turk. We will tack for the bow of the galleass, and at the last moment possible, shift to fly past her stern. We will be under heavy fire from arquebus, Culverins, and arrows. We are also all aware that we have a good supply of bow and arrows, ourselves, but what we have in number, we lack in skill, and rest assured, the enemy will have many more missile weapons than what we have at our disposal. The sea-worthiness of the brigantine is what matters most, for without such we will never outrun the enemy, but in the same token, we have to ensure ourselves of our survival in order to escape to safety. We cannot have one without the other. I have therefore devised a plan which is sure to help us in this predicament." Stephen commenced to pace the deck as he spoke, the entire throng listening with baited breathe, and their very lives hung in the balance... rested within the hands of this young knight. Stephen had come to defend Constantinople, and now he was a commander, a man in charge... in control. "We shall cut away a portion of the decking, like the slits of a knights helmet, so that we can lie in wait beneath the deck, ready with bows in hand. I will position you all personally, and we shall rehearse our attack. We shall fire our volleys through the opening within the deck and kill as many Turk as possible, without bringing fire to bear down upon ourselves. Direction of flight can be directed easily enough, but many volleys must be placed into the air in order to allow the good sailors of this boat to steer her away from danger, when the time is ripe. With the wood we cut away from the deck, we can build a little structure about the helm, to help provide protection and cover for the sailors so stationed. No one must be exposed to the Turks' fire for any more time than is absolutely necessary. Only, and only if the Turk sends marines, or other ravenous dog aboard our boat, will we meet them in hand-to-hand. Lars, Lois, and Andrew; station yourselves within the cabin, cut a hole from which to deliver your quarrels… on either side, for port and starboard could have equal exposure. Everyone else must be prepared to provide sustained volleys with the bows. Once we have steered well away from direct assault upon the galleass, those firing the bows can prepare themselves as required: to either sally a boarding party, or help with the sails and rigging. Catherine will advise as to direction of flight, left and right, up and down; she will watch from a makeshift hole within the boat's side. She will have a spear in her hand, one that she has used so professionally in the past. This she will hold this parallel to the hull, holding the point of the spear in the direction of the enemy target. Toran, Anthony, and all other able bodied man, must be prepared to fight with sword in hand, and if you have no sword, and one cannot be found, then find yourself something pointed and sharp that can inflict such heinous injury to the assailant, that such a sight will make even the toughest of billygoats puke. If you wish to see the sun rise tomorrow, you will heed my warnings and ready yourselves accordingly. If you wish to see another day born, do what has been requested of you," for Stephen wasn't quite ready for the feelings associated with giving-an-order. Far too many times had he seen commanders ignored, or spoken of poorly behind their backs. He wanted those around him to appreciate his command and structure; he wished all of those around to be comfortable with his presence, as he was with theirs. "Master Andrew?"

"Yes sir," came the solid reply, Andrew growing ten inches taller with the call to recognition.

The Templar addressed the small crowd then: "Stephen will be fine, Andrew: for all of you here, I am no more deserving of authoritative obedience than anyone else. I am at your service, more than you are at mine. I do immensely appreciate your admiration, but we are all friends here," he looked to Andrew once again. "I think we need to attend the woman with the broken leg, but when time to fight arrives, she must be made comfortable and left to tend herself. I, and Father Norotus, shall see to her injury soon," and to the crowd. "If anyone here needs to speak then the time is now, for the fight will be upon us soon."

"Aye," said the sailor Fabian, known little, by few, for he was contentedly busied with sailing the brigantine. He held up a cloth, some fabric, and a myriad of colours. "I have something, found in the captain's chest below... I was not intent to steal..." and his stance sank miserably, "but a little wine to wet my throat. But I found something, Stephen." The sailor held it up for all to see, as it unfurled and flowed to the deck of the boat beneath their feet. It was the flag known by all that watched, the Imperial Eagle and Lion of Saint Mark.

A smile formed upon the Templar, as too with others around. "Hoist it immediately," said Stephen, "for we have been without flag for far too long." A few tears welled here and there, others looked up proud, some even slapped hard the back of the person beside them. They still had a sovereign identity and their hearts were as proud today as ever before.

"Abu, Abu!" Ibrahim ran into the cabin, where his commander was lying at rest.

He jumped immediately, upon his feet in a flash, his hands fumbling around for his sword. "What is it?"

"The Christian brigantine has raised a flag, the Imperial—"

"You what? You great oath!" Abu turned half-on, indicating the bed of blanket upon his table. "I was sleeping comfortably... I said I was not to be disturbed unless..." and he shook his head and hands. "Forget it Ibrahim." He sat heavily and picked up a quill – but not through any real necessity. "Is that all, Ibrahim? Is that all you have for me?"

"Yes, for the present."

"How far is the boat now? A league or more."

"No, Abu, just under a league," and he was stunned that Abu could not be bothered to open his eyes and window shutter to look upon the Christians himself.

"Watch them carefully. I want that boat, Ibrahim, and all aboard it. It would do us all well to prove of our ability. Who knows, maybe I shall receive a promotion on return to our glorious lands."

"And I, Abu, would like to serve you has I have always done," but within his exoskeleton of lies and false servitude, Ibrahim did hope that he could be released from his chain through the death of his commander; but his death would have to wait for a promise of treasure was lurking. "A return to Constantinople would be grand indeed."

"You fail to look, to where... as others I have met, are too scared to look; for I do not wish to be shackled to a bedpan, when a garden of rose and petal awaits me in other lands of opportunity."

"But the opportunities in Constantinople, Abu; too good to pass on; so much power is to be taken... it is all for you, Abu, if you should be willing to pick it."

"What, like fruit from a tree?" said Abu. "No, Ibrahim, it is far too much work, for someone as ambitious as I. There is far too much waiting for me in other cities, that all I need do is take my choice from a basket already prepared: why waste time with picking and cleaning? Although, I do admit, sometime will have to be spent in the city of filth."

Ibrahim dared to daydream then. "Many servant girls will be waiting, ready for a man, breasts filled with that sweet scent of..." Ibrahim stopped himself from further drivel, for his eyes met

Abu's, his commander staring insult and ridicule into him. "But it is your decision, Abu. I am sure you will be happy. As for me, I am but a humble servant myself," and with that he bowed slightly. "If you will excuse me, Abu, I shall be on my way."

"Yes, be on your way, and send me news as it arrives," Abu waved Ibrahim away. "Go, do what you do, and do it quietly."

"Yes, Abu, thankyou."

Syahid appeared at the hatch, holding onto the rim and ducking his head low, to see inside. He gave a nod, received well by Abdullah.

"Muhammad, look. Syahid has something."

"Good, Abdullah. Let us see what it is that is worth the attention of our ears."

Both men made way for the hatch, departing their station below the forecastle, their accommodation amongst the more worthy of the slime within the ranks or oarsmen and marine. They clambered upon deck, squinting against the bright light of the sun above. It was easy to see by the shadow cast upon the deck that it was midday, and their stomaches called out for a morsel to satisfy their hunger. Abdullah pat his solemnly; "Wait my beloved, for I shall feed you soon."

"Abdullah, Muhammad; here, quickly," Said Syahid.

"If there was a prize for discreetness, then it would be yours, Syahid; for I know no other that can be as eluding as you," said Muhammad sarcastically.

Syahid smiled, the derisive comment having gone by his intellect. "Thankyou, Muhammad but listen to this. I have heard further talk, of Abu's intent to return to Constantinople with his prize once his venture has been fulfilled. From there he seeks promotion and retirement."

"Who cares what he seeks: but still, that's not good," said Abdullah.

"No, not at all," agreed Muhammad. "If the men get their promised ransom and rape, we will have little choice but to return to Constantinople, for the men would have received fulfilment."

"We need to continue with our quest," added Abdullah.

"Indeed. The secret of the brigantine must be ours... to share amongst others, of course; especially you, Syahid, for without you we would be lost."

"Eternally," said Abdullah, adding open sarcasm where it was not clearly understood.

"No, we must act soon. We must seek favour from Ahmad, and we must do it now. If we are to soon be engaged in battle... tell me Syahid, death in battle is open to all, not dealt to particular individuals, but to all men. What if we could arrange for Abu to be struck by an arrow?"

"Or a sword," said Syahid with a smile.

"Yes, indeed; or with a sword. Are you up to the task, Syahid? Do you think you can do it?"

"What? Kill a man? Kill Abu?" asked Syahid, almost stumbling over his words given in a soft whisper, as he looked over his shoulders.

"And why not?" asked Muhammad.

"He is 'the strangler'. How can I kill someone so treacherous?"

"Syahid, listen to me. He is only treacherous, for the men he commands. He only gives orders... it's others who act on his behalf."

"He is weak," added Abdullah.

"Indeed," concurred Muhammad. "What do you say Syahid; Ah? We are all responsible, are we not? And you haven't yet been party to any part of our plan so far."

"But, Muhammad, nothing yet has been achieved."

"And I shall soon see to that, Syahid. Please, you go do what you need to do, and we shall see to the rest. We have to get some men on our side in order to lay influence upon the others. There are many oarsmen who would like nothing more to see a sharp knife dragged across my throat."

"And mine too," added Abdullah.

Syahid was quiet for a second or two, but nodded acceptance of the task. "I shall arrange for his... parting."

"Good; good man. And we shall see to the rest."

Syahid approached one of the men, known quite widely as an assassin... of the past. His name was Hassan. Now he was considered nothing more than a poor wretch, who took orders to directly appease his needs. Rape wasn't easy to come by in old age, and although quite young he wore many scars upon his face, one of which was a burn mark of considerable size, covering from neck through to forehead, a well-defined line between scar and flesh drawn down between eye and nose on the left side of his face. He had lost several fingers on his right hand, so was useless as a swordsman – of any description – though quite good with the bow, for the three fingers most in need for operating such a weapon were his greatest asset, and his legs ached when he walked – it was once said of him, that rape was no longer possible, for a scared women could run faster than he could, especially when he had his belt dangling down around both knees and with his hand on his manhood.

"Hassan, please, I wish to speak with you," said Syahid with the greatest of respect, for his request could well spell his own death.

Hassan turned abruptly, a look of disgust falling across his face, as though something rotten had been placed in his mouth. "Syahid, I don't speak with scum, and you I loath." Hassan could see something was up, however, for Syahid looked to his left and then his right, and also, through the corner of his eye he could see that the coxswains were going about some business and did stare in their direction... with a smile upon their faces. "Tell me your need, for I have work to do."

"Work for pittance?" stated Syahid.

"What are you saying, Syahid? If there was not too many eyes around I would strike you down where you stand."

"Hassan, I agree with you: I am a scum, a scum of the earth."

Hassan's thrown upon his forehead pushed down upon his eyelids, confusion in the answer throwing Hassan from frame of thought. "You are? Of course... yes; you are a scum, Syahid... but... Don't trifle with me, Syahid. Tell me of your needs... or question, or whatever it is your want from me – I have business to attend: quick about you... quickly I say."

"Many riches, enough to fill your pockets ten times over," replied, Syahid, thinking that such an answer would appease, Hassan's greed.

"Ten times... how many is that?"

Syahid looked the man right in the eye, an unblinking condemnation of Hassan's stupidity. "It is more than you can fit into your pockets, ten times over... it is enough to fill your pockets, again, and again, and again, and again, and..."

"Enough, enough," exclaimed, Hassan, throwing up his hands. "You are telling me it will make me rich beyond all my dreams; is that it?"

"Yes!" Syahid thrust a hand to his mouth, quickly lowering his voice. "Yes indeed, enough to fill your needs for the remainder of time. You will be so rich as to afford yourself ten... many, many wives."

"What is your need; explain? You have my attention; and quick about you."

And as Syahid commenced to explain the need for cooperative-coercion, he saw Abdullah and Muhammad talking with three villains.

"I told you Syahid would do well to serve us. Hassan is a good choice," said Abdullah.

"I agree," Muhammad was still smiling from the scene, Syahid talking with Hassan. "And there," he indicated with a nod, "is our first port-of-call."

Boabdil, Abdar, and Hamed – surprisingly enough – were parleying upon the aftcastle of the mahon, looking out at the brigantine as it made its slow journey down towards them. Muhammad saw Abdar look towards him as he closed the gap. Muhammad smiled and said to Abdullah, quiet as can be: "It looks like three at mischief."

"So long as they serve our need, I care little," replied Abdullah."

And as they came within earshot, Abdar greeted them. "Ah, our good friends, Abdullah and Muhammad. What brings you into our good company?"

"Your personal reflection upon your character as a group, is unwavering in truth and conviction, to say the least," came Muhammad's reply.

"Such praise spoils us." Abdar laughed. "We are looking to the treasure of flesh, which currently comes towards our starboard," indicated the man, unnecessary as it was. "I ache for the feel of a woman right now, more than mortal man can endure, I tell you. We should all be in Constantinople right now, cheating the nuns of their virginity."

"I think we all agree with you," said Muhammad, as he and Abdullah arrived at their side. "But we must make the most out of what we have."

"And that won't be much," said Hamed.

"I agree," Abdar said, nodding his head in acknowledgement of the truth. "For how many women will there be on the brigantine –

surely not enough to keep 120 fighting men contented and spent of energy."

"No," said Muhammad, "you are correct in your assumption," and then he lowered his voice, for below where they stood was the sunken quarters of Abu. "Which is why we seek your assistance."

All three looked to the two men having just joined them, crowding in on the conversation about to take place.

"We have known each other for a long time, have we not?" asked Abdullah of the three.

"Yes," agreed Abdar, looking to the others.

"We are good friends," Boabdil smiled.

"Indeed," Muhammad made a fist with his right hand, pounding the air, inciting truth, and bringing the urgent need for call to action into the open. "We must consider our position. We all know that once the brigantine has been taken, and three days of pillage – so ridiculous…"

"As to be insane," said Hamed.

"Quite right," and Muhammad continued: "Why; by the time we get to Constantinople, there will be nothing for us."

"More than likely, nothing already," remarked Boabdil with a miserable look forming upon his face.

"We must act now," said Abdullah, indicating his support for Muhammad.

"The brigantine is full of treasure," said Muhammad. The other three looked at him in wonder, regarding the information, considering whether it was true or not. Muhammad simply nodded. "Do you see Syahid, down there, speaking with Hassan?"

"Scum," said Boabdil.

"Both of them," insisted Hamed.

"Yes," said Abdar, "But you have something, don't you, Muhammad?"

"Yes, and I agree, they are both scum; dogs of this world. But we must use what we are dealt. We are intended to be rid of Abu, but we can't do so without the necessary support."

"You mean us?" said Abdar.

"Indeed, yes; but Syahid is apart of the plan… we can be rid of him later," and Muhammad smiled, the grin of satisfaction becoming contagious, and the mention of treasure was just too good to be true.

And Abdar asked the question that was on the others' lips: "What kind of treasure?"

Syahid didn't need to express too much detail in regards of the required 'accident'. And so, as Hassan and he departed company, Syahid decided upon attending the talk, which was still taking place upon the aftcastle of the mahon. He could see quite clearly that the conversation was thick and fast, many smiles and slapping of shoulders taking place. All appeared overwhelmed with the plan to execute Abu and the attractiveness of the treasure. Suddenly the boat approaching from the gauntlet of the Dardanelle could be seen, quite large but approaching slowly, seemingly drawing out their demise and final death. Syahid set to find Ibrahim, to have Abu notified accordingly, for the sooner they were at battle, the sooner his plan could be hatched.

Ibrahim took the news from Syahid and listened closely to what he had to say, before preparing to wake 'the strangler'.

He stepped into the confines of Abu's quarters, the sound of his placing a bowl and jug of water upon its place waking him. He stirred slowly and then leapt to a standing position.

"You have news?" the sleep was still encrusted around his mind, clear thinking kept at bay.

"The Christian boat is close now, Abu; it won't be long."

Abu turned and peered as best he could through clouded eyes. He rubbed them again and looked upon the sails of the Christian vessel with better clarity. "Into the lion's den they do wander. A great victory this will be; an easy victory." Abu turned with a smile encrusted upon his weathered face. "Go upon deck, Ibrahim, and set all to alarm, for the time has arrived to man the oars and ready ourselves for battle."

"But one thing before I attend your flock, my esteemed Abu."

"Ah; what is it? Quick about you."

Ibrahim looked left and right, suspicious; "Something of great importance, Abu, something which is worth much gold, and my purse is very light."

Abu looked his personal servant up and down, seeing nothing more than a peasant in ragged clothing, and not a messenger of any worth, and that alone intrigued him. "You have me interested, Ibrahim, but the time is not—"

"The time is now, believe me," interrupted Ibrahim, "for I have news from Syahid."

The five conspirators saw Ibrahim exit Abu's quarters, departing as Abu attended the washing of his face. Abu could hear his words of command, passed from Ibrahim to the crew, the clutter of feet upon the boards of the mahon drowning out the pleasant flow of water as it cascaded from the jug, a handsome measure of water being poured before he commenced with dipping his hands into it, and splashing a little upon his face. He turned amongst the noise of the action above, to look out upon the Christian boat through open portal as it gained ground upon his trap: and such a trap it was, but the other, that was more important.

"To station! To station!" yelled Ibrahim as he left the solitude of Abu's quarters behind him. "Man the oars, marines to post, archers form rank!"

To the five conspirators, Ibrahim passed on the orders as though from Abu himself. They quickly drew his attention, like food thrown to a passing gull in flight. As he made is approach the three men, Boabdil, Abdar and Hamed, departed company with a quick nod of their heads, Ibrahim falling disappointed that the congregation had fallen short, his eyes following the departed; his prying would now go unfulfilled.

"Your orders have frightened away our folly of friends," said Abdullah.

"Time for action has arrived, the Christians are coming."

"Yes indeed, I see the sail has been placed high and she tacks well for an escape."

"And if she tacks again it will be for an immediate assault," returned Ibrahim.

Both Abdullah and Muhammad could not contain their laughter, Muhammad taking the floor with appraisal of the situation. "And an easy task that would be, my good friend, like a mouse taking on a lion. The skill of a tactician you have proved to behold."

Ibrahim smiled within for he could feel wealth flowing through his fingers, as though poured from a carafe.

"If they attack, they are dead; escape is their only hope," continued Muhammad. "It is obvious if you don't have the sense of worm and the sight of a bat?" and the hurt within Ibrahim's eyes was seen quite clearly. "Forgive me, Ibrahim. I meant not to tax your wretched mind; we all have a place in this battle to come and yours has been fulfilled;" and he looked again, deep within him. "Even if it be a simple command."

Ibrahim departed with sulking features and as he did so Syahid came in from behind the pair, their attention gained.

"Ah, Syahid," announced Abdullah, "How fares the masquerade."

"Quiet, Abdullah, you are too free with your voice," replied Muhammad.

"And you forget yourself too often: my friend."

Muhammad took the chastisement as it was and looked to Syahid. "What news do you have, and quick about you?"

"Muhammad, Abdullah, I cannot tell a lie," both comrades smirked at this, "for I have sealed the fate of Abu like no other."

121

"Well done, Syahid; I knew that you would," said Abdullah, "and it would seem that the time has come for us all to attend our stations, for the calamity of battle will yield the fruits of our mischievous rebellion."

"To war!" yelled Abdullah and attended his post with quickening stride.

It was time for battle, the Christian boat closing on the galleass that sat there, motionless, at full sail and a myriad of sailors with hands on ropes ready to rip the anchor from the channel floor. The sails of the Turk boat were stressing, the ropes creaking, the boards and rafters moaning like a whore after too much wine and horizontal pleasure. Many men remained unseen, hidden behind the walls of the boat, along the decking between oarsman and upon the fore and aftcastle, as organised by Mouley and Ahmad. The coxswains, Abdullah and Muhammad looked upon the forecastle from their station, staring at Ahmad, the puppet-to-be, unbeknown of the change of command which was about to befall the crew.

"Ready I hope you are, Muhammad?" queried Abdullah.

"Ready to beat the oarsman to death, if I have to," and a few of the sailors at oar, closer than most, turned their eyes upon the coxswain who was as careless with his words from mouth as he was with his cadence from drum.

"The sails," Syahid pointed towards the Christians. "So close I could spit upon them."

"Ready yourself, Muhammad," came the advice from one coxswain to another.

"And you too, my friend."

Stephen was there below deck, looking upon the slit above, the boards removed for the perpetual delivery of arrows upon the heathen Turk. He had stationed all hands, personally; it was a refinement of his previous orders to ensure that they were victorious in escape; he had done all he could. And he looked around more-so, completely begotten by the courage of Drusilla, the woman with the broken leg, for she had insisted on being stationed with the others and was at present opposite line of her comrades in arms, to the task initially appointed to Catherine: to position a spear, up and down, left and right, directing the arrows for the median delivery of the bulk. She rest with her back against the hardwood of the boat, leg stretched out in splint, bound in cloth ties to hold the ensemble together. Catherine, standing upon a barrel, had her eyes glued to a small hole in the boat's side, horrified to the closeness of the enemy, which even now drew closer. She turned her head momentarily to see Stephen standing beside the archers, he too with bow in hand and sword scabbard at his side, his weapon of choice ready to be drawn. She received a warm smile of friendship and confidence, her task cemented, and the belief of her ability strong within all around, eight bows against a crew of unknown size but estimated to be in excess of 120 sailors with detachment of marines.

Fabian, Eben and Jacob, the sailors three, crouched as low as they could, behind the makeshift shield of boards on deck, the main sail of the galleass almost blotting out the sun, but certainly half the sky. They steered their quarry of fighters to allow for the flight of arrows to hit their marks, after feinting to the port.

Abu saw the move to port and was quick with his order.

"Anchor now! Oars to rear, pitch to starboard! Drop the mainsail!"

Muhammad the coxswain beat the skin of his drum, slowly at first, the oarsman applying the necessary manoeuvre to endeavour ramming the Christian boat as the mahon sailed rearward, the dropping of the mainsail allowing for faster control, for the wind was blowing from the south. The words of command were exactly that and acted upon with the quickest of ease. Abu smiled but was horror struck with the clarity and suddenness of his error. As the first volley of arrows from the Christian boat came flying through the air, from the unseen enemy below deck and protected well by the boarding of their vessel, the sailors aboard that damn vessel steered obstinately to starboard, away from the implemented ramming.

Abu was dumbstruck, hit hard by the change in tactics. The Christians weren't trying to evade him by turning behind, but heading for the bow. He couldn't believe his eyes. "The sail, get it up, get it up! Coxswains, all ahead... oarsman... damn; full-ahead!" he then saw Syahid meet with Hassan and disappeared back to his quarters.

Catherine returned her gaze upon the galleass: "Ready!" she yelled.

Drusilla repeated the command, "READY!"

"Fire!" "FIRE!"

124

Eight arrows were released; six made range, one missed, and other yet had struck the inside of the boards above their heads, Toran shameful of his skills, though a man-of-his-craft when it came to fighting hand-to-hand and with the sword in palm.

"Elevation good, slight left!" "ELEVATION GOOD, SLIGHT LEFT!" and the spear in hand was shifted to Drusilla's right, the appropriate change in direction applied there on the line of archers looking upon her as she faced them. They continued to place arrows into bows and eyeballed the woman with the broken leg and steadfast Catherine, Catherine, as though born to command, gave an order to the third in line: "Dorothea, higher!"

"DOROTHEA HIGHER!" came the confirmation from Drusilla.

Lars, Lois, and Andrew; stationed within the cabin, set upon to fire their quarrels as targets revealed themselves. Their speed had seemed to increase, an optical illusion drawn upon by the galleass drifting rearward. Targets were made all the more easy to set upon now as men ran around putting adjustment to sails, trying effortlessly to hoist the mainsail which had been so easy to lower. Lars felled two men in as many breaths, Lois and Andrew slower to get in their aim.

Mouley, commander of the marine detachment, fell short of ordering the firing of his weapons; for use was a culverin against the boards of a boat; it was flesh he wanted to see revealed, and as for Ahmad Kadir, little opportunity their was for him with no target revealed except to fire blindly with a mass of indirect fire that he currently held in reserve for chance targets that may appear.

The reservation aside, he gave the order: it was passed down the line of archers, each stationed between the benches hoarded by oarsmen, putting ready their bows upon linen strings, applying the pressure required to pull back and bend the bow, to release and see hurtled upwards a darkening mass of arrows, points glinting in the sun as it continued its trek into the afternoon.

Syahid came up to Hassan, hidden by the excitement of the fight as it commenced to unfold. "I see you have your weapon ready."

"As promised, Syahid. I hope that Abu can pay as you have put mention."

"Don't you worry, Hassan, for to help with the killing of Abdullah, Muhammad and Mouley Bakar, you will be handsomely rewarded."

Hassan turned with mixed emotion in his eyes, forehead cringed, upper lip shifting with the hate as it grew within him. "You said nothing of Mouley Bakar… his men are—"

"Weak, Hassan, very weak. They would follow Abu as quickly as a whore will undress before you." He held his hand out, taking hold of Hassan in a gesture of good will and friendship. "We will do this together, Hassan." He indicated with his eyes for Hassan to follow in gaze. "Look over there, who do you see?"

"Ibrahim."

"What does he have in his hand?"

"A knife, it seems…"

"It is." And Ibrahim looked over to them. "He is ready, Hassan. Watch closely."

And as he watched he saw Ibrahim call Abdullah over to his side, to be called into Abu's quarters during the calamity of all on deck.

"He calls him to his parlour, his mansion of death." Arrows from the Christian boat fell all around, shots from crossbows hitting their target, and a single flight set flame to the sail above their heads.

"Ibrahim; the fledgling of cowardice; he calls Abdullah?"

"Yes, Hassan; he calls him to his death. And now we must ready ourselves. When Abdullah disappears into his oblivion I shall skew

Boabdil Ali and you shall kill Mouley first and Muhammad second."

"What the hell is going on, Syahid. Are you the devil?"

"Hassan, listen to me. I have promised you riches beyond your wildest dreams and now… it is time, look, Abdullah retreats with Ibrahim. The time is now." Hassan gave to hesitation. "You are not a coward, Hassan, I know this. Do as you have been asked and you shall be rewarded."

It was then that Hassan smiled and cocked his bow ready, and as Syahid brought Boabdil, leader of the three, so fond of Abdullah and Muhammad, to his death, Hassan killed Mouley and Muhammad in less time than it takes to have a piss.

Calamity grew all around and it was good that the lives around them were taken in the order they were, for the falling of the first took attention away from the others, and for the few that had gathered around the dead it seemed strange that those killed were struck with arrows fired into their backs, not from the enemy on the starboard side of the boat.

Arrows continued to be the answer to the call of battle, until the last of them had been spent. Around 80 arrows had been fired in such a small amount of time that it was hard to fathom. Stephen stood erect amongst the cries from the galleass, heard as men hurried about their business and the burning of the sail.

"To arms, all of you. Take your weapons and be ready to meet the pirates so willing to course us the heartache we feel so strongly after the fall of Constantinople. Gather your spirits." He looked into the eyes of those below deck, seeing firsthand the valour instilled within each.

Abdullah stepped into Abu's trap, with weapon sheathed and in a flurry.

"What is this, Abu? Commander you may be but the time is.... Gluuuuugh." And the knife in his back was twisted left and right, Ibrahim's hand lifted Abdullah's mouth and nose, to aid in the death of their quarry.

Abu came close to gloat over the dying, Abdullah's body falling limp, being allowed to fall to his knees.

"Your time has come to pass: poor Kadir, how you will be sorely missed for your wit, or rather, lack of it," and he continued on past, towards the entrance. "Throw his body out through the bow, be quick about it."

Abu stepped into the fight and his first instinct was to see his bidding complete. The bodies of the slain settled him, but the sail ablaze, high above him, set him into motion.

"Abdar, Hamad! Abdar, Hamad! Here as quick as your legs can carry you," and it was well orchestrated. "The coxswain has fallen, take his post, both of you."

"Where is Abdullah?" asked Abdar.

Abu looked him in the eye as he settled upon the station. "Question me again, Abdar, and I shall see to it personally that you are flogged to within an inch of your life."

"Yes, Abu, but I see—"

"Guards!" two men soon rallied at Abu's side, brandishing swords. "Take this filth away, chain him below."

"No, Abu;" he looked to the guards. "Sherif, Mollet, NO! You know me, both of you."

"Gag him if you must. Now take him; quickly! And then return to station."

"Yes, Abu; immediately," answered Sherif

"Hamed, do you question me?"

"No, Abu."

"Then set about it, you pile of filth." Abu saw Ahmad Kadir working feverishly about the oarsman. "Ahmad!" the commander of the sailor detachment heard the calling and lifted his head to a new command. "Hooks; to the hooks."

Three oarsmen dropped the paddles they were sworn to sweep and set upon the hooks positioned along the length of the mahon. The Christian boat was being steered well by the few sailors aboard, too far out for hooks and bridges formed by planks, but nevertheless, would be given a go. Sailors swung the cumbersome triple-headed hooks above their heads, only one of the three in any position to grapple with the Christians' escape.

The hook flew through the air with such expertise and landed upon the deck, drawn backwards with the motion of the two boats and the pulling action of the sailor with the hook's rope in hand, until it found a niche and held its position, secure and ready for a boarding party of marines to assume its command over the battle.

Andrew looked out, distracted by the movement of the sailors and saw indeed that the hook had a good grip of the boat near the aft of the vessel, the sailor pulling it taught. He aimed his crossbow and let loose with a shot, the arrow missing its target but hitting another. It was then that Stephen came out from his peripheral and seemingly dodging the arrows being fired at him, and the culverins so haphazardly employed – as though God himself was watching the knight's task – did hack down with his sword to cut away the rope from the hook; he fell then out of site, away from the danger of the missiles that continued to be fired towards him.

The Christian boat was pulling away from the galleass, with its main sail set ablaze and the coercion of the oarsman seemingly lost for good. Stephen could only hope that no extra sail was stored below their decking for the replacing of the old cloth to take place.

Syahid slipped away as Hassan turned," The job is… where are you to, Syahid."

"To task; question no more."

"I shall seek my reward."

"NO!" he turned upon Hassan. "Do you see the battle, it still rages. Wait till later you fool."

Hassan scoffed silently to the name calling and felt the burden of containing his anger, but control it he must if he were to be rewarded. And then, from out of the blue, Abu called to him.

"Hassan," the assassin looked up. "To me, quickly." The joyful man of misguided mind set upon the order as Abu continued with the regaining of the initiative, but it did not come. The sails above continued to burn and the chase would soon be lost. No supply of cloth existed within the confines of his glorious mahon, and so, until a friendly boat did pass, the opportunity of a lifetime would have to be put on hold.

Syahid soon arrived upon the scene where Abdar was placed into chains, locked tight to one of the many vertical beams within the hold. The guards were conversing amongst themselves, upon the delivery of Abdar to punishment, of Abu's disciplinary sentence upon the newly appointed coxswain.

"It is to the battle that the blame should fall," said Sherif.

"Abu needs all the men he can muster, to send us down here with Abdar is not right," replied Mollet.

"It is a warped mind that has ordered me to chains."

"Shut up, Abdar," spat Sherif. "You shall receive your chance to speak, but until then you can just shut your mouth."

"Ah, Sherif; Mollet. How fares the criminal?" interrupted Syahid.

Both men turned to stare. "Syahid, you filth. You startled me," said Sherif.

"Me too."

"You too, Mollet. That doesn't seem too hard a task."

"What is your insinuation, Syahid?" questioned Mollet.

"Nothing more than the fact that I know well of your failing courage at times of need."

"That is uncalled for."

"But very true, Mollet. Any normal man would have had a palm at my front by now, or in the least, a knife drawn to disprove the accusation." Syahid watched the man Mollet who turned to briefly eyeball Sherif before returning to the deck. "I have other duties to perform... not to waste my time here when a fight is raging above our very heads." He disappeared from view.

"You were wise not to have accused me, Syahid, otherwise you would be dead already," said Sherif, non-too deterred by what had just happened.

"Yes, but now we are alone. I was hoping this would be the case." Syahid looked at the prisoner chained to the beam. "It seems that Abdar is one of three conspirators."

"Conspirator? I swear—" Sherif kicked the man hard and he sulked into quietness.

"You see, Sherif; you too have ambition, courage, and the need for gold."

"And pillage," Sheriff smiled, "don't forget that."

"Indeed. I believe a Wiseman once said that a gold coin in the hand was worth two women in the bush."

"That depends on the bush."

"May be the case, Sherif, but I can tell you this much: treasure, beyond your wildest dreams is yours for the taking, but you must follow my orders, and those of Abu's, without question or fault."

"But my question would be, what treasure?"

"Upon the Christian boat." Syahid looked down upon the foetal form of Abdar and spat. "Kill him."

131

Sherif nodded in quiet acknowledgement, for he knew of 'the strangler', and for he to have ordered Abdar to chains, in time of battle, and when no real cause to do so had presented itself, meant that there was good reason: Abdar was a conspirator and Abu was a great tactician. There was many things that a man learns about another, in particular of those that hold higher station, and in particular of their past. Abu meant to keep his word, but only where unquestionable obedience went without fault. Sherif was a man of men, war and pillage were his calling, gold was his need, and killing someone as pitiful as Abdar meant nothing more than stepping upon a rat to cave in its head.

The shrieking from Abdar was quickly held at bay by the big hand of Sherif. He saw Syahid disappear from view and understood well that something was afoot, for he had seen the arrows bedded deep in the backs of those on deck.

He drew his knife quite deliberately; allowing the horror to sink deep into Abdar's mind, for killing was Sherif's pleasure. The point was held against his neck, and quite slowly, still with the torment of a hideous smile, Sherif pushed the knife into Abdar's windpipe. He released his hand now, holding his palm against Abdar's chest in order to restrict the body from thrashing about and he quickly choked in his own blood.

The night had arrived and none too soon. The Christian boat had escaped with little to no damage and the mahon had been crippled with its sail burnt to a crisp. The dead were delivered to the sea with little to no ceremony of any great worth and the men took to rest and water as they waited upon the waves in the narrows of the Dardanelle's.

Abu had stationed several sailors to watch for a friendly boat as he, himself, had taken to the deck of the aftcastle, looking out upon the water to the east. The sun had almost disappeared beyond the horizon in the west, a striking red sky dominating the night air. A sailor then called from atop the crow's nest: he had sighted something. Abu looked out again, straining hard to see over the waves as they rolled the mahon up and down each crest. And there it was, as far in the distance as could possibly be; a boat in full sail of triangular shape. Abu smiled, satisfied. He turned upon a new task, to immediately ensure that extra lanterns were set, in order to gain the attention of the other mahon as it closed the gap.

The fight had been won, the Christians victorious, and a new day had been born unto the small band of men, women and children. It was the day after their escape and the sun had reached its highest point. Stephen was sleeping below deck, for he had refused to allow himself the creature comforts of a more humble station as normally provided a captain. Homer was dead and forgotten; all except his legacy, his urgent and most sincere need to reach Káros. And so the brigantine continued its journey towards Káros, the sea calm and friendly, the wind favourable, and the sun out in all its glory. And as the goings on of the boat continued a voice came to Stephen has he slept: Do not rejoice in victory over your enemy, but forgive their grievances against you. This is a covenant of your Lord. The battle of the day before then came into his dream, the one-sided victory overturned, to such a degree that the brigantine was swamped with a thousand men, and as his precious Catherine was about to be raped by a heinous Muslim with gnarled-rotten and filthy-dark teeth he was woken by the sweetest voice... "Stephen, Stephen."

The Templar opened his eyes, shuddering slightly from the dream, and there before him was Catherine, holding a bowl of gruel, a luxury soon pushed aside. "Good morning, Catherine; well you are, I hope?"

"I would be better to have my troubles accepted." And she pushed the bowl back into his hand.

"The others are more deserving."

"The others know that you have been going without your share. They all know this to be true. Besides, we are fewer now; the Turk boat is gone and we have favourable wind to the south. Fabian says that we shall be at our journey's end within a few days."

"Fabian?"

"He gives command to Eban and Jacob," she smiles and laughed, "and they follow his orders like a true captain." Stephen smiled too and then thought on the reality of the situation with a prompt from Catherine. "But we all know who the captain is, Stephen. Why do you sleep down here, in the cold and damp air?"

"Am I more deserving that I should be of warmer station whilst women and children suffer below?"

"No one suffers, Stephen. Everyone is on deck as we speak"

"You know what I mean. Go upon deck, Catherine, and order that Drusilla be taken care of in the captain's quarter. You and Lois can tend her needs; stay with her." Catherine looked blankly at Stephen. "That is an order, Catherine, and it would please me to see it carried out." She stood fast looking upon his now seated form. "Do this thing for me, Catherine, and I shall eat your gruel." She smiled and departed without further word.

Catherine entered the quarters, where the Priest Norotus had set himself comfortable; he was on his knees.

"Damn you child. Don't you see I am in business with the Lord?" He got up from his knees and felt pity where pity should be felt. "I'm sorry, Catherine. These past few days have been hard for me... for us all."

She shrugged her shoulders, caring little. "I come with word from Stephen."

"Ah, and what is the word?"

"Lois and I shall tend to Drusilla, here in the captain's quarters. All else must pitch a pellet below."

"He said that, did he?"

"Yes; it's the only way he'll eat his gruel."

The priest gave a mocking, stern look, seeming disgruntled but calm. "Well, forbid me to unset the appetite of a king!" He pointed his finger heavenward. "I must leave at once."

"He's only the captain."

"Yes, child; I think we all know that."

Norotus entered the darkened hold, quite aware of Stephen sitting upon his blanket of straw.

"I see that Catherine has tended her task."

"Yes, Stephen; and might I say how amused I am about it all. There's not much room down her, is there, barely enough to stand tall."

"For a man who spends the best part of his day upon his knees, preaching to the Lord, I see no reason why space should be a problem."

"I am but His humble servant, that is true," said Norotus jokingly. "Where can I plant myself?"

"Here, next to me," and as he sat, Stephen asked a question. "Father, I had a dream—"

"Don't tell me, a voice."

Stephen smiled. "It came to me as strong as any of the others."

"And what did He say to you?"

"Do not rejoice in victory over your enemy, but forgive their grievances against you. This is a covenant of your Lord. "

"Ah. Well it seems to me that you may be feeling guilt upon the glorious victory we have won. It's easy to forgive those that have not the advantage to take life. The victory you won for us was indeed a miracle in itself. But also: that a victory should not be rejoiced for it is not yet complete."

"But it is written in the bible, I know this verse, heard it before. You were apt to believe me yesterday."

"Stephen, listen to me. I doubt you not, that voices have come to you and that the chest may have everything to do with these... visitations; but it hard to see why the voice comes to you and no other. Why not to me?"

"I cannot answer for the lord, and nor do I question."

"Forgive me, Stephen. The fall of Constantinople has taxed me heavily. I trust you have been chosen for a reason... I just don't understand why."

"Did you read the letter, the letter from Constantine?"

"I have read it."

"Do you believe it?"

"I believe the chest holds... something; a mystery perhaps; a sign from God."

"And of baptism," asked Stephen, "is it true that if you house evil within your heart and mind that you are impure?"
"I believe so."

"And that if you are not baptised then the power of the chest has no power over you?"

Norotus looked Stephen in the eye and pondered the question.

Stephen continued: "If a man of Muslim faith has not received baptism then he may not be affected by the chest; although he is impure he has not made an open oath unto the Lord."

"And the devil will reside within him," and the priest was stunned by his comment.

"A Muslim cannot be swayed by the chest, father, for he has never been baptised. Hear me, father, hear me now. 'Do not rejoice in victory over your enemy': this is because the enemy is the devil and resides in all, therefore, although a personal victory has been won, the devil resides in others, the battle forever waged. And further still; 'but forgive their grievances against you': we must forgive them as individuals for the impurity of heart is not of their doing, but that of the devil. Do you see, father, do you understand? We do not fight the Muslim Turk but the devil, the impure; we wage war against hell itself."

"There is only one way to find out, Stephen. The chest must be opened, at all costs. If what is to be revealed will indeed deliver Christendom into eternal hell then it must be hidden for the remainder of time, never to be opened again."

"And as it has been mentioned before, father, how many times in the past has it been opened? Why is it that the key has been kept so far from the lock? Why is there nothing recorded on the contents of the chest, other than what has been provided us via the passages recorded by Constantine and his predecessors?"

"These are questions that must be answered. Once the answers have been provided to us we can then, and only then, decide on the fate of the chest."

The days unfolded without incident, islands being passed as they continued their voyage towards Káros. The days remained calm and the wind in their favour, the brigantine being tacked well to gain that little extra knot in speed. At one stage they came so close to the island of Psará that it was most difficult indeed to abstain from landing, even for the shortest time. Tínos to their port, Míkonos too, but it wasn't until Náxos came into view that many hungered deeply for the brigantine to be taken into port. A few smaller vessels could be seen jollying around closer to harbour, and several insisted that they could even see the figures of people running around upon the shore. No boat was launched against them and they continued on past, course set for Káros, a few hours away.

When Káros finally came to view it seemed to be a hostile place indeed. Twice as wide as it was across, a half days journey by foot, either way, was arduous indeed. To cut across the land was to pass over its mountainous terrain, a steep climb followed by hazardous decent, even with the aid of the manmade track that zigzagged both up and down the monstrous terrain; travelling lengthways was just as difficult, for the jagged terrain of boulders and buttresses of rock forced detour upon detour to be made.

The sea was calm enough for all to enjoy their approach upon this unfamiliar island, even Drusilla had been provided a sitting station from which to look out over the sea and towards the approaching land. She thought then of the hardship which was to follow, of the burden she thought she would become when others would have to carry her over such hardened ground, but this sinking feeling was soon washed aside for all could see the murky darkness of a wall take shape and there, amongst the buttresses of rock formed over centuries past, tall towers that seemed to launch themselves out of the rock itself. It was a castle, a monstrous castle built into the island, the walls shaped along its base to meet that of the land around and the walls encrusted with merlons between its four towers. The closer they drew to the island the clearer it all became, such a fine line between the colour and consistency of the rock of the island and the stone blocks of its defence; this, they all knew, to be their objective.

Stephen looked up to the lookout: "What do you see, Eban?"

"Very little, besides that castle. It looks evil; very evil."

Fabian came alongside Stephen. "And what if they are?"

"This is our destination. Fear no evil."

"Are you a preacher now, Stephen, because you sound like it?"

"The only evils here are the ones that follow beyond our wake, and the one we have yet to bear witness to."

"Is that a riddle?"

"No, Fabian, it is knowledge of the quest, a quest which has yet to be revealed." Stephen looked into Fabian's eyes and understood

138

his calamity, for so few had yet been advised of the chest and its heavenly secret. "Gather everyone, Fabian, even the lookout from above, for I have an announcement to make, something to tell all that will change the way in which they think."

"Yes, Stephen."

All had gathered around the centre mast of the boat, its course set towards the castle of stone upon a fortress of rock columns and buttresses. Stephen stood before them in his hose and undershirt, well-quilted vest and chain mail with hood. His sword in its scabbard of wood rest against his left leg and his dagger remained strapped tight in place. So much of his personal possession had been lost, abandoned, or given up to the hungry waves of the sea; he looked like a knight of light purse and no horse, of little importance: but such appearance can be deceiving.

"You have all been gathered here so that I may make announcement." A few flinting eyes pondered, for it appeared that what was to be provided their ears would quench more than their individual need for information. "Some of you already know of what I am about to reveal, but those that do: their identities will not be revealed to the others, for it would go unfairly against them that others might feel... uncharitable towards them." And the eyes all fixed upon Stephen. "From the time we first set sail from Constantinople, this brigantine has been setting its course for Káros. To the then-majority it was the belief that such a move towards a safer station should be embraced, in particular when considering our situation and other friends so close to call, in Náxos and other lands, which at times could be touched by an outstretched arm as we sailed past them. But there was good reason, and that reason is about to be revealed to you... you would do me proud to refrain from asking questions.

"Much has happened upon this boat, so much in fact that it appeared to be too coincidental. A conspiracy, a traitor, and being run down by Turks upon their galleass. Torture has been exercised, burials at sea. We have waged battles, and won." A cheer went up but Stephen help back the high spirits with his upheld and open palms. "Please, please." Silence was restored. "We have passed many islands that could have provided us with sanctuary, fresh food and water, and we have set ourselves a goal: Káros. And what of it? You see in front of you this minute. Dark and evil, a mountain of rock; a castle upon a fortress, seemingly so impenetrable and forbidden that even the Sultan with his monstrous army would see to pass it by rather than to waste the time to sack it for its pittance worth of treasure or reputation." All looked out momentarily to the castle upon its foundation of rock. "But that island is all important. It holds a key, a key guarded by a small army of Hospitaller knights. The knights of the hospital defend the castle and its treasure within, a treasure that does not bring wealth, but knowledge and security. The key within those wall so high will fit the lock of a single chest and within that chest is a secret of biblical proportion, a secret which may never have been revealed before to the society of man, never before in the history of human existence has anything more important been laid at the foot of the Christian religion. But something more I must tell you, and that is the chest to which the key has been born is upon this very boat... yes, I tell you the truth. A scripture from Jesus, or message from God, I do not know; but I know this: whatever will be revealed to us when we enter that castle of the hospital, the very one that stands before you upon that mountain of rock, will be for the betterment of all. I know you will have questions, but answers I cannot give. Even I have much I wish to ask, but to whom do I pose the question? We must all wait for what is to be revealed. I ask now that you all attend your station and prepare what belongs and weapons you can manage to plunder from this good boat, for we may or may not have the opportunity to return, for the Turk could well know of our destination, thanks to a few that have already been delivered into eternal rest."

As the conglomerate of friends approached the shore they saw, not a station for which to pitch their boat, but jagged rock with the power to smash to smithereens all that they owned.

"It would seem that your friends of the Hospital don't take lightly to visitor," said Norotus, looking out upon the shoreline, the gentle swash of the sea ebbing in and out upon a small escarpment of sand between buttresses of rock. "I can only assume, from what I see, that they accept their entourage by why of rowboat, and little else."

Stephen took little time in thought and pondered no more the calamity to be avoided. "We must gather the men immediately; to get as close to shore as possible and use what barrels and other materials we can to salvage ourselves, ourselves alone."

"And the chest, Stephen."

"Of course, needless to say that the reason we are here is to protect the unknown."

The men worked haphazardly as did the women and children, Catherine always close to the heel of Stephen and Lois close to Lars. Empty barrels were taken from the hold and brought upon deck along with other materials to be lashed together. The distance to the shore was short and the sea as calm as could be expected.

The time to anchor was soon upon them and the iron hook was lowered unceremoniously into the sea, sails unfurled and persons readied for their excursion into the unknown.

Norotus drew up alongside Stephen, a cross held in his palms, clenched tight against his chest.

"Are you praying for our safe passage?"

"I am praying for courage."

"What need you of courage? You are a priest; in the eyes of the lord you can do no wrong."

Norotus paused to answer, which he did in a low whisper. "I do not know if I am pure, Stephen. It might be that I have had secular thought."

"You, father?"

"Yes; I."

"I would not worry if I were you. I am sure that there is a difference between action and in-action."

"I hope you are right."

Stephen slapped Norotus on the back in friendly gesture. "I'm sure I am," and to the surface of the sea he looked, the row boat, and barrels and planks lashed together, put into the water.

Eben and Jacob, under the guidance of Fabian, took to securing what luxuries they had to the makeshift raft of barrels and planks, the chest taking centre stage and secured firm.

"How goes it?" asked Stephen.

"Almost ready for the landing party, Stephen."

"Let me know when." Stephen turned to Lars. "Ah, my good friend. I would ask that you be the last ashore, along with the women. As soon as I am ashore with Fabian, Anthony and Toran, I shall send Eben and Jacob back with the boat. Send the children next, and you too, father."

"Aye, time enough to give prayer."

"For more courage?"

"No, Stephen. For you and your landing party; look." Norotus pointed off into the distance, upon the shore of the island to their front. "Look to the thin tree line, between the buttresses of rock. I see some men."

"Ah, yes. I see them now." Stephen turned to Lars. "What do you think?"

Lars nodded acceptance, a small smile upon his face.

142

"I agree." He turned to Norotus. "It is nothing."

"But men all the same, hiding amongst the trees."

"A welcoming party, father. If they meant us harm then we would not be able to see them. They don't intend to ambush." Norotus was obviously troubled by the sighting. "Pray for the chest, for our future depends upon its contents."

"Stephen, we are ready!" yelled Fabian.

Stephen turned to carry on with the task at hand. "I shall see you ashore, father, and you too, Lars. We will have much to do once within the walls of that castle, and much food and water to dispense with as we desire."

The remainder of the boat's crew of men and women gathered around, to see the row boat head for the shore, Stephen, Eben, Jacob, Fabian, Anthony and Toran, the first to step upon Káros.

Norotus looked to Lars and gave to a suggestion that made him ill-at-ease. "It seems to me strange, Lars that Stephen should choose to go ashore with able-bodied sailors and two mercenary. If my eyes had their way I would believe that an ambush is exactly what Stephen will meet; and how are we to fair then, with a crew of women and children?"

Stephen kept his eye on the party ashore, two men dressed in black. Fabian watched the depth of the water as the other four rowed. "I see our friends are knights of the hospital; I see the white crosses upon the tunics as easily as I see the shore to our front."

The two knights came out from the shade in which they were standing and commenced to walk towards them. They stepped with purpose, not slow and deliberate, not with haste or action, but a pleasurable stride with arms in motion, hands well away from the swords they carried. Their heads were bare, no mail could be seen; other than the swords at their sides no armour was worn.

"They are friend, not foe." Stephen turned to look upon the boat behind, the others watching with patience, even the woman Drusilla had positioned herself to see the meeting between the knights and their landing party.

"They seem friendly enough," said Norotus. "It is good I have this cross around my neck. To be without it would be to drowning in the sea of panic."

Andrew, the ten-year old from Constantinople looked upon the priest, who was almost as tall as the lanky boy. "Its okay, father; you can stand behind me if the meeting turns ugly, for my sword is your friend."

Norotus met the boys glare and patted him on the head. "Good lad, someone to count on if the need arises; I feel better already."

The barrels and plank bobbed up and down as and the shore was finally met, the chest being dragged ashore, proving to have been kept dry, and the crew stepped from the row boat and panned out to meet the two knights as they approached.

The knights smiled and Stephen was forced to do the same for a friend should be regarded in a similar fashion.

"Good men, I am sure," shouted the first knight, "from where do you come?"

"We come from Constantinople, and my name is Stephen."

The knights held out their hands as the distance finally closed between the two parties. "Ah, Stephen." The first knight introduced himself. "My name is Edwin, and my companion is Bastion;" and both smiled extensively, "Bastion because he fights like ten men."

All shook hands.

Stephen introduced his comrades in escape. "I have with me men of courage and a tale to tell. I have here, Fabian, Eben and Jacob, sailors of grandeur which I am pleased to serve with, and two men of unbelievable stature, Toran and Anthony: they both fought with the great Giovanni."

"Ah, Giovanni, a great man indeed, we know of him," agreed Edwin.

Bastion looked to Stephen, "And what is the news of Constantinople?"

"It has fallen," replied Stephen without hesitation.

The two knights looked upon one another in shock. "Do you have many others with you?" asked Edwin.

"A few women and children... which we must secure before we continue; please forgive me."

"Not at all, Stephen; a captain must do as is demanded of him."

"Please, Eben and Jacob, untie the chest and see to the others."

"At once, Stephen."

Toran; Anthony, please wait here a moment," asked Stephen of the two mercenary. "Please; Bastion, Edwin; may I," and Stephen stepped with the two knights to talk a little on the subject of key and chest, and of the fall of The City of God. They, all three, walked the short length of the shoreline. "It grieves me to advise that Constantinople could not be defended. The walls were breached after many hours of constant fighting, Mehmet replenishing his tired men as he so desired, whereupon the Christian, so few in number, tired and bore the brunt of constant attack from right around the perimeter. I tell you both this: we were lucky to survive."

"Stephen; you seem troubled, as though the burden is yours alone," said Edwin, he being taller than Stephen, scars upon his face numerous, no stranger to battle himself. "But let me tell you, the burden is for the Pope, and his miserable efforts to provide help when needed."

"Do you receive news of the Aegean often?"

"We are but 100 knights of the hospital that remain stationed here for a reason, and yes, news of the outside world is delivered on a weekly basis. And I say this too you, Stephen: You are not simply here because you chose to be. There are many islands between Constantinople and Káros; you didn't just happen here by error alone."

"Yes, indeed. You are right, Edwin, and I think you know what I have."

Bastion answered: "We know the chest by sight, Stephen; we have seen drawings of it. We know of the chest which currently rests upon the shore, guarded by your three men." All looked back down the beach, Eben and Jacob almost back at the boat, the two mercenary and Fabian standing fast where they stood. "Do they know what the chest holds?"

"They know all I could tell, but even I am lost as to its contents or meaning, and I..." Stephen trailed off.

"Please, Stephen; what else do you know?"

"It is hard for me to speak of some things."

"You are amongst friends. You have voyaged here for good reason; you follow orders, orders given by way of Constantine – that is the only answer," said Edwin.

"You are right; I was forgetting... I will tell you something that only a few others know, and that is of the voices."

"Voices?" question Edwin, stopping in his tracks, the walk temporarily brought to a halt. "What do they say?"

"I have to report three, and I remember them as clearly as when first heard: they roll around in inside of my head as thou lost and looking to be found." Stephen looked the two knights in the eye. "The first is: He who breaches the bounds of my scripture; he shall be delivered unto everlasting contempt. This is a covenant of your Lord."

"We know of this one," said bastion.

"Do you know what it means?"

"First, tell us of the others."

"The second is: Greater love has no man, but he who surrenders life with good cause. You will not see decay when delivered unto the Lord. And there shall be no prejudice comparison between servant and master, for no one is above the Lord. This is a covenant of your Lord." Stephen paused again and they continued walking. "The last: Do not rejoice in victory over your enemy, but forgive their grievances against you. This is a covenant of your Lord." Stephen requested an answer: "What can you tell me?"

"I tell you this Stephen, we, both, know of two, but not the third verse, that one we do not know."

"I thought that the first was quite simply: to abide by the scriptures or be damned."

"Not the most poetic way of putting it, Stephen, but nevertheless quite accurate," said Edwin.

"I believe the second to be as simple as the first, but the third... I have spoken with our priest—"

"You have a priest on board?" bastion seemed excited by the announcement.

"We do, but please don't see too much into it; he is as lost as I am."

"That is not good, Stephen. We need help with this; religious instruction."

"And of the third verse?" questioned Edwin from Stephen.

"I can only surmise. I did think that it was meant to be deciphered, that the meaning is hidden within the verse itself."

"We have had trouble with deciphering these voices too, Stephen," announced Edwin.

"You hear them too?"

"Well, not me, but a friend of the hospital. He is a lay priest of no singular importance, but he can be trusted; he has helped us with much... You simply are proof to what he has been saying over the past few years."

"Not that we don't trust him," interrupted Bastion.

"No, of course not," defended Edwin.

"I think the third verse is an announcement that the Turk is not to be feared in as much as what he carries within his mind and in his heart... but that the devil resides within him. His religious faith protects him from adhering to the other verse, hence a man of Muslim faith cannot be judged by the lord."

"Yes, indeed," they all looked up to see that they had almost returned to the row boat, which itself was making its final trip back from the brigantine.

"We must talk more on this, Stephen, but for the moment we must retreat immediately to the sanctuary of the castle," said Bastion.

Edwin followed the gaze of Bastion back to the castle wall where three silhouetted figures could be seen holding standards of red.

"What is it?" asked Stephen.

"Three galleass travel this way, enemy boats to be sure. I am sorry to say, Stephen, that even as careful as you have been, you have been followed. The enemy is now pressing this way. By nightfall we can expect to have anything from two hundred to four hundred enemy camping on our doorstep, and we are but one hundred."

"One hundred and sixteen," corrected Stephen as he looked upon his band of men, women and children.

"I like the sound of your courage. Get your people ready, we move shortly." Edwin turned to Bastion as Stephen moved out of earshot. "My good friend, as soon as we are in the castle I wish you to dispatch a knight to the orphanage. Make sure you brief them accordingly and don't frighten the children."

"Yes, Edwin. It is as good as done."

The group of twenty moved with eagerness towards the hidden entrance of the walled castle, an entrance easily seen once revealed, tucked away behind a small rock formation. It was quite obvious to Stephen that the entrance saw little commercial use of any description as it was as small as a sally port; any army trying to enter through it could be cut down at will, one man at a time and with little effort. The mortar of the castle walls was an inch thick in most places, holding together the moulded defence, each brick seemingly cut to shape from the rocky surrounds. The only thing that allowed the castle to stand out against the ground around was its shape.

Bastion was the first through the doorway, it being opened from the inside. The door creaked heavily as he pushed from the outside and a knight from within grunted as he pulled.

Bastion entered and stepped aside, his left arm extending upwards in a fanning motion, inviting Stephen and his crew unceremonious entry of the castle. Each went in through the doorway in single file, Toran and Anthony porting the chest, which had been shrouded in cloth. Niketas and Fabian carried the woman Drusilla, and Edwin taking up the rear. Stephen, as for the others, looked around the infrastructure of the castle as they entered, many building attached to the inside of the wall and a large temple to the centre-rear. There was a metalsmith and several larger dwellings that looked like barracks, and another, which from first appearance looked like a buttery and later proved well to be their storehouse for keeping food and drink. A large stable with several dozen cows, pigs and goats, and a henhouse with chicken run took up the remainder of the space along the inner walls.

Bastion entered last and helped the other knight close the door behind them, it being secured by large planks falling into place across it, and Bastion briefed the man of the requirements as laid down by Edwin. And even now, as the group of twenty commenced to form as a small crowd, Edwin gave introduction to the surrounds, a quick sentence or two on each of the building around: "...and through that little port over there, to the right of the temple as we look at it, is where we grow our harvest. The ground cannot be seen from the shore, from sea, or even the mountain trail that leads up and over the side of the mountainous terrain of the islands spine, but it is quite vast to which the Lord gives special favour. And last of all it is my great pleasure," and a man dressed as a priest could be seen to approach, his hood being pulled back from his head with a smile, "to introduce the only man of the clergy of our establishment, who holds all responsibility for the food we eat and the prayers we give, the man who holds the key to our existence," to which Stephen and Edwin locked eyes momentarily, "Father Tourmede of Vallencia."

"Ah, my sons and daughters," his smile was contagious and he shooks hands with every single soul as he spoke. "I am so pleased to meet you all. Strangers you may be, but in the face of the lord you are children of his heart and members of His flock." He came upon Norotus and spoke to him deliberately before continuing. "And you are?"

"Father Norotus, a priest of Constantinople, Saint Sophia, fourth in line to the Abbott."

"It is grand to speak with you. Sup with me you must, before with give praise to the lord for his bountiful gifts."

"It would be my pleasure," and he kissed the back of Tourmede's hand as delicately as could be.

Father Tourmede was summoned to Stephen, standing beside Edwin, Tourmede having deliberately allowed himself to overlook the important looking fellow for an extended conversation. Edwin said: "And here is Stephen, father."

"Stephen; soldier I see dressed before me, but something more is hidden behind the masquerade."

"A knight," spoke out Catherine. "Knighted by Constantine himself, for the courage and valour suited a true Templar Knight."

"A child should not speak—" Tourmede interrupted, but was himself scolded for his unacceptable behaviour, and by Stephen.

"The child is Catherine and is free to speak as she sees fit. She has saved my life and is as bound by the scriptures of my once Order, as I was once affiliated."

"A knight, not a knight... a Templar?" questioned Tourmede with an ounce of scoff.

Catherine stepped up to side herself with the Templar. "He is a knight, a Templar as true as you are a priest to the church. He is free to choose how his body of flesh should best serve its purpose, free to govern his actions as his mind desires."

Tourmede looked down upon the child, though tall she was for her age. He had noticed, without mistake, how all others had fallen silent – so the girl was of high character and status. "I stand corrected: Catherine," and to Stephen himself, "a Templar knight, such status would be hard to prove... but I am not in the position to ask for such." Tourmede looked straight into Stephen's eyes, who had not moved an inch and had remained steadfast without emotion portrayed upon his face, a look of command having fallen over him, a look of honesty, courage, honour and bravery shown by the way in which he stood. "But I know of this: you have come this way by no accident, to beach yourselves upon an island of rock with no harbour; in particular where you boat seems to be in good order. You travel from the North and have passed many islands which would have welcomed you in open arms," and Tourmede turned his head to Edwin and asked of him: "So what is it with this man that should be known, Edwin?"

Edwin looked left and right, unaware as to what should be said in line with the question. Was it not Stephen who had pulled him and Bastion aside, to walk the shore and converse on the chest, the key, and the verses from Him? If Stephen was to speak behind the backs of those he had journeyed with, maybe there was a reason. "It would be best to refresh our newfound friends with food and water before departing on such a... what could be an extensive interrogation." And Edwin's eyes told the story, Tourmede

151

understood the message, and Catherine was concerned over the word 'interrogation' and put her arm around Stephen, protective.

Stephen put it all to rest and comforted those around him with words of encouragement: "I must agree, we must talk further on our situation and immediately so, as suggested earlier by the knights standing guard upon the walls. All must be refreshed."

"Please, this way, one and all," announced Bastion. "This way to our kitchen." And the crowd, some unsure, some needing further persuasion, and still others requiring no further word, shuffled off to the building second only in size to the temple itself, to be fed like kings and queens, to be watered like a thirst-driven flower of the desert regions near Israel. Drusilla was carried and the chest too, was taken.

So Edwin, Tourmede and Stephen were now detached of the others. "You are mysterious, to say the least," said the priest.

"If I may," said Edwin. "I believe all things will develop more quickly by revealing a few... things." Tourmede's eyes had proved his interest, and Edwin continued. "Stephen has a chest with him, father, and knows of the voices."

"Ha ha ha ha ha; music to my ears. I knew there must be good reason for your being here." Tourmede stepped closer, put his arm around Stephen's shoulder, and all three walked off towards the Temple. "Forgive my show of friendship, overbearing it is at times, but to finally meet with another, from outside of these walls who has heard the verse; I must say how relieved I am." They stopped suddenly before Tourmede released his hold on the knight and they continued their slow walk. "How much do you know of the chest, of the verses, of the secret to be revealed?"

And Stephen told his story as the three walked towards the temple and steered to the right, towards a simple looking building, which was none other than Tourmede's private quarters, large enough, as it was proved, for a table from which to seat six and a bed for one – the most humble of all creature comforts Stephen had seen provided any Priest, monk, or other member of clergy; and the conversation continued as a plate of food was taken and tumblers were filled with the freshest of water Stephen has ever tasted.

"This water is very good."

"It comes direct from the mountain," answered Tourmede, "just another gift from Him; and speaking of Him, you have said that you are troubled by 'hidden-meaning'?"

Stephen pushed his empty plate aside and took another gulp of water. "The verse: Forgive their grievances against you..., and more still, as I have said. I think there is meaning here, more than can be seen... or heard. Please, allow me to continue. If the Turk is not guilty of such a savage belief then blame must be with the devil himself. Why? If you house evil, you are impure; if you are not baptised then the power of the chest has no power over you; if a man has not received baptism then he will not be affected by the chest for he has not made an open oath unto the Lord. The unbaptised cannot be swayed by the chest. Father, we wage war against His opponent, not against those of Muslim faith."

"I see it all now," said Tourmede, "and I believe this to be true;" and it seemed, for the slightest instant, that Tourmede was hiding something from Stephen. "Every word you have spoken makes good sense."

"So," prodded Edwin. "What does this mean? That the chest should remain locked forever?"

"I don't think so," said Tourmede. "I for one know that I am pure."

"When were you baptised, father?" asked Stephen.

"And what does that matter?"

"Humour me."

"As a young boy. I was taken in by nuns, a lovely little convent that helped the needy and brought up orphans."

"So you had little choice in the Baptism?" Stephen was hunting.

"No, not true; I was asked and gave permission, nothing was denied me," answered Tourmede. "But I don't understand how this as anything to do with one's faith," was Tourmede testing his faith, testing Stephen's true allegiance?

"Don't you see, father. You were of an age where you did not fully understand the requirements of the Lord."

"Are you saying that I am false, that I should not be considered Baptised?"

"Yes and no; I don't know. But if you were baptised at an age where understanding was at its greatest, and you, for some reason, had impure thought or impulse of any description, then, and only then, the chest could have an adverse effect upon you."

"I cannot believe this for an instant. You are telling me that I might be impure. You call me a liar to my face."

"Father, listen to me; look at me, please." Their locked eyes. "Do you house the devil?"

Tourmede could take no more and stood abruptly a fist banging upon the table, Stephen's tumbler falling. "This is absurd. I will not be spoken to in this way."

"Do the pure condone outbursts like the one you have offered me this minute?"

"You would deny Christ, would you not? Would you not lie to Him, bring Him down; make Him feel as sick as I. You are not a Knight of the Temple, you are not a man worthy of that Order; you are not worthy of the dress which they wear, which I might add is why you are not wearing the Lord's cross upon your chest right now."

Stephen too, stood. "The reason I have none is for good reason, but I know where my faith lies, and if you should be tempted to open the chest then it would be my duty to talk you out of it, even if I believed it should be done. I long to see inside, like any other mortal man, but I don't wish to see an evil escape whereby the world of the Christian faith, be it Orthodox or Latin, crumbled upon the earth as cinders from a fire place or hearth."

Tourmede looked to the Hospitaller. "Edwin, call for all able knights to be housed in the temple within the half hour. We shall see what the chest has to reveal."

"You are making a mistake, Tourmede."

"So we shan't see you there, Stephen."

"I shall be there, father, and I shall have all others of the boat in which I arrived given the opportunity to savour the contents of the chest. I hide nothing, from no one, and wish only for the sanctity of our religion."

Norotus had adjourned to the private quarters of Tourmede where a small library of religious virtue covered the dusty shelves along two opposite walls. Two knights carried the chest behind them.

"Please, place the chest there and continue with your duties." In silence the knights put the chest down and departed.

"My dear, Norotus. I am happy that you could see for yourself a little of my library. It is unfortunate to say that it might be lost to the Turk's flames of purification, and this entire castle with it, for although a nice little stronghold it does make, has no real strategic importance. Please, take a seat."

Both sat.

"Norotus; we are both refreshed and have little time to talk, so I shall get to the point and rather hastily – I hope you will forgive my poor lecturing ability."

"With so little time available, as you have mentioned already, I, too, feel that courtesy at this time should be forgotten."

"Good, then let's get to it." And Tourmede wasted no time at all in allowing the information to flow. "The chest just there, yes, the one that brought you to us. I have the key and it shall be used as it should, to open the chest in full ceremony," said Tourmede, quickly adding, "but in accordance with the time we have left."

Norotus simply nodded.

"The inscriptions upon the chest, let us write them down."

"No need, brother, for I have a list, penned aboard the boat during our days at sea."

"Ah, Brother Norotus, so humble it is to meet someone with the intelligence to plan ahead. Let me see."

And so it came to be that the information within the library provided some answers and a majority of the inscriptions upon the chest could be deciphered for what they were: messages from Christ.

They poured themselves over the books, gallantly paving their way through passages of text, through verse and psalm of praise, prayer and sermon, until the time was upon them to cease with their work. Although it was fair to say that not all was understood, it was clear to both that the chest held a secret, one that was to promote the Christian religion to its rightful spot amongst all others, that the truth would be revealed upon it being opened, that faith would be restored unto the human race.

A guard of ten Hospitaller Knight stood upon the defence of the walls as the boats of the enemy draw ever closer. The three galleass appeared to have put to rest just off shore, close enough, it seemed, for the captains of each to plan their strategy before flooding ashore and laying siege to the castle or in conducting a hasty assault. The remainder of the men, all ninety, surrendered themselves to the opening of the chest. Of the fifteen that came ashore with Stephen, all had requested to be present during the ceremony that was to take place later that afternoon.

Norotus had made proper preparation and had spent a little personal time with Tourmede, the two conversing heavily on the chest, the visible inscription, and the character of Stephen. It was with them that the heavy burden did rest for it was within the knowledge of all that the Turks were currently planning their heinous activities to supplant them all. Norotus was provided much information but due to time available permitted his patients to take seat and await the opening of the chest which was to occur before time ran out.

So it was that Norotus found himself seated within the tiny space of the chancel and Tourmede upon the altar as the Hospitaller moved in to be seated behind those already in attendance; namely those from the brigantine. Stephen was last to enter with Edwin and before they did so a few sentences passed between them.

"Stephen, I must have your ear."

"I am listening, Edwin."

"I fear the fate to befall us all, even in the light that the chest is to reveal something grand to us, the Turks will be here soon enough. This castle will hold long enough, but it isn't for me that I fear."

"If you say the castle will hold then I believe you; a little time is all we need. The Turks will evacuate and return with larger numbers, I am sure of it."

"That is to be seen, but nevertheless, if they were to climb the mountain, to navigate around it or gather better vantage of the situation, they could well come across the orphanage."

"The orphanage... I think I heard it mentioned when upon the beach. Tell me about this orphanage?"

"On the other side of the mountain there is a very small harbour, far too small to be seen from the sea, and without knowing the currents within the inlet no man would dare attempt a landing... but I am drivelling. There are nuns upon this island who take care of some orphans. The responsibility for them fell upon the sisters just a few months ago, and the nuns converted their quarters into a home and a school for the children. They were rescued from a shipwreck, hostages of the Turk who sought to take harbour upon our island. We slaughtered all of the men as they swam ashore."

"How many children?"

"Shortly, Stephen." Edwin could see that time was short for the last of the knights were seating themselves. "The children are between eight and ten years of age, and all are girls."

"The Turks—."

"Precisely. They will stop at nothing to rape the nuns and the children. The misery that will fall upon them is unspeakable, as too is the misery that they have already suffered."

"You must send a detachment, immediately."

"The nuns were notified, not long after you arrived. We have time. I have given further orders to be advised when the galleass commence to deliver their cargo of sailor and marines. The trek to the orphanage is only short."

"Surely, they would be best brought back here; we must send for them at once."

"No, Stephen. The harbour, behind the rocks there is a boat, a carrack large enough for the children to make good their escape. There are eleven children altogether and the carrack will only hold twenty... possibly one or two more, but with supplies... I fear the worse. More than that is possible but not desired." Edwin could see the look in Stephen's eyes. "You understand, I see you do. You must take no more than six good men with you, eight at the most, the carrack will not support any more. Rations are being loaded this minute. No matter what happens here you must withdraw and protect the innocent."

"I shall, Edwin."

"Good man, Stephen; now let's take a seat and await news on the Turk's landing and let us see what happens when the chest is opened."

"Wait! What about the nuns?"

"They have done their duty, Stephen, they are henceforth in His hands."

The two men seated and the service commenced, and although a long and deserving service was preferred by Tourmede, time was not on their side.

And the thoughts of what was to come swamped Stephen like the plague.

The activities just off shore commenced to take shape. Tactics were the call of the day, for both the Turk and the Hospitaller Knights. If the Turk were to be victorious then quick action was called for.

The knights watched from the high walls of the castle and could see with good clarity all that was to befall them.

There was much activity upon the deck of the centre-most galleass as supplies were being moved to the other two boats. All manner of crates and barrels, no matter how small or how large, could be seen, being moved along the lines of sailors, over heads, passed from one man to another, ferried to safety, and within the half hour it dawned upon the Hospitaller guard what was to occur, for a small crew of men boarded the now ransacked galleass and brought her in closer to the shore where more man power had accumulated to pull the hulk of wood and sail up onto the silky sands. Craftsmen with tools in hand commenced to pull apart the boat, every piece of wood being torn from its mother, each piece being salvaged for a new purpose: for the purpose of war. The Turks were pulling apart one of their boats, to employ the wood in the craft of battle, forging scaling ladders and other apparatus for the shielding of men with bows. Archers would now have a defence to hide behind as they delivered their arrows, and the marines would have ladders for which to scale the walls of the castle upon the rock known as Káros.

All the guard upon the walls could do was watch in anxiousness. It was clear to them now. These Turks had a purpose and would not stop until they had succeeded in their task. They now had only two boats and too many crew; what choice would they have but to succeed in the fight, and with the loss of life would arrive the available space upon the galleass to ferry the sailors and marines back to Constantinople – if in fact that was their destination.

The guards upon the wall looked at one another, waiting, saving the precious time they had remaining. They all understood, from the work being conducted upon the apparatus for war that they would all die, but they would not give their lives cheaply. They served the lord their god and would not forsake His name for the opportunity to brief in a dozen more breaths before life was extinguished. Their purpose in life was to protect the key, the very key that was about to be inserted into the chest, a token of hope delivered from Constantinople. Even in death the City of God was calling out in victory, to make a final stand against tyranny, to voice to one and all that it would not give in, would not die, and would fight forever and a day. What was mortal life to the Hospitaller but a prelude to eternal existence, where every day in heaven would be worth one hundred here on earth.

And Tourmede looked upon the seated forms of those that had congregated for the service, the ceremony of opening the chest, and after having given much praise and psalm the key was handed to Norotus, for the pleasure would be his. Norotus had indeed delivered the chest to Káros, it was now his duty to open it, to reveal to the world the secret of its contents.

Silence fell and the key was inserted, pushed into the chastity of the keyhole, a perfect fit, and as suddenly as they key was inserted the voice fell once more upon the ears of Stephen: Love your God with heart and soul so each is of equal measure. This is a covenant of your Lord. And the meaning of the verse was as clear to him as was the figure of Norotus to his front; and the chest was opened for all to see; and the meaning was this: That purity of soul was no more important than the knowledge of Christ, that one cannot be achieved without the existence of the other. Religious life could not be ordained without both existing as pillars of truth, where the temple of the body must maintain such beliefs and not waiver in the slightest. If impurity of heart existed than a balance between knowledge and spirit did not exist; securing knowledge of Christ was not as significant as being pure. Allowing oneself to praise the lord with impure heart, or to house an impure heart with sanctity of knowledge... they could not exist with equilibrium, could not co-exist: for the devil was at home and brewing revenge.

And the calamity of the truth behind the verses fell from heaven and the congregation heard the earth quake and the air rumble. Norotus looked in upon the chest and a brilliant light burst from within, blinding him instantly, for the impurity of his soul was damned by his actions upon the multitudes of Constantinople, for when in sight of the church he did condemn the innocent, who were pure of heart and mind. The shock of the sight brought screams to air, people averted their eyes and presented forearms as shields – and the light spent immediately, but the screams and stammers continued.

The shock of sight and sound brought a panic, the once seated were now standing, or down upon their knees praying for forgiveness, but a handful of men, women and all the children did not see the blinding light, did not hear the rumble in the air, nor feel the quake of the earth; what some saw was a miracle in itself: the Holy Spirit did transcend from the chest, a smile upon its form, and it sped off into heaven, through the very roof of the temple in which they sat.

But the upheaval in some continued without a break in the horrors being seen and felt, where the ground around them vibrated their very souls, and each grabbed for their throats for they were being choked, their very life being drained from within them.

And as the Holy Spirit disappeared from view a voice fell upon the few in such sweet undertones that all the horrors about them, was denied them. They did not see the choking, could not hear the last sounds of mortal men and women drown from existence, for the voice of the Holy Spirit was delivering to them a message, something so sweet to the ear that it had to be heard to be understood.

Alas, Stephen saw none of this, for his purity of heart and soul were so sound that the truth of his surrounds were seen for what they were. He looked around calmly, not in shock, not in awe. He saw the majority choking to death, clasping for dear life, he saw the minority, in particular the children, looking with wanderous prose upon the chest, where their eyes moved upwards towards the ceiling above them, and the voice commanded something of him, one more voice which was yet to play its part in his immortal existence, for he could not die. And the voice dealt upon him the following verse: He who sounds the trumpet at time of war shall be provided sanctity in heaven. This is a covenant of your Lord.

One of the knights burst through the door of the temple shouting out with all his power, "Alert, alert, the Turks—," and what he saw brought him to his knees, as there before him were many dead, sprawled across the pews and in the isles, and the sight was sickening and could not be understood. Other knights then, the purist of the pure, raced to give aid to those that were already dead, though calm they were in action. The knight so recently assembled looked down to his right and there he saw his commander, Edwin, death having been delivered unto him.

Stephen took command of his senses and turned to the sound of the alert. He called out franticly. "Get out! Get out now!"

The knight got up to retreat but was too late, for the earth rumbled and the air shrieked with its call to death, and the man choked, his hands grasping at his throat for clear understanding. Stephen shook the occurrence from thought and took further command. He had to collect his thoughts, he had to calm the emotion within him, but most of all he had to take stock of who was present within the temple and still breathing, for it was they who could be trusted above all others, for they were pure.

He looked firstly to his comrades and friends, those of the brigantine – thou least important, for all of those that had journeyed here with him were present at the opening of the chest, so all of those alive were indeed pure, but the children, had they been saved?

He could see Lois of eight-years and Andrew of ten. There coming to view, to be cradled by one of the surviving women, Lucia, was his Catherine. He saw Dorothea and then Lars; the others were dead. And of the ninety knights that were present at the ceremony only Bastion and five others could be seen providing a helping hand. Stephen looked up finally to see the priest, Father Tourmede of Vallencia, and although Tourmede should bear great responsibility for what had just occurred, he was without mistake as pure as the rest.

"Father!" Stephen called out to the priest. "Father! Wake up, look to me!"

Tourmede lifted his head and eyes to see Stephen walking calmly towards him.

"Your duty, father, it to seal the chest, before more men come walking through the entrance of the temple. It must be sealed, father, and quickly if you please."

Tourmede fell from the dais upon the altar and raced down to the open chest and without looking in, for fear of his life, closed the chest and turned the key, withdrawing it from the lock and placing it within his pocket.

Stephen drew alongside the kneeled form of the priest. "Did you see inside, father? Did you see what no other mortal man has ever laid eyes upon?"

He looked up to the templar, wiping tears from his eyes, mixed tears, some of fear, some of sorrow, others of happiness. "No, my Son, I did not look into it. My courage did fail me."

"Don't worry, father. It is clear to me, and should be to you, that so long as we are in the presence of one another, the chest may be opened at any time."

Tourmede stood up. "I think not. We should try and decipher the inscriptions fully, then, and only then, should we endeavour to disturb the spirit within."

Stephen smiled in agreement and turned to all within the temple that were now standing, waiting for a command.

"There is no time for speeches. Some of you know what had been delivered us, and there are those of us who do not," said Stephen, looking to the children in particular. "But we must gather ourselves and make our escape. There will be time for deliberation later, but for the moment we must withdraw to the orphanage and prepare for evacuation. Does anyone here oppose me?"

Not a word was spoken until Bastion called to attention all of those waiting for a protest. "We, the knights that remain, are hereby at your disposal, Stephen. I wish to further advice that there is a secret pathway through the mountain, from the rear of this Temple to the rear of the nunnery. The climb within the cave is cruel but efficient, made easier by a solid path of steps. Of those that remain only I and Father Tourmede know the way." Bastion looked to Tourmede. "I ask you, father, to deliver these good people, and the knights that remain, to the orphanage on the other side of the island; take the chest with you. I shall brief the men on the wall and remain with them."

"We need you alive, Bastion," called out one of the knights.

"No. You have Stephen and the others. The children must now be cared for. Besides, we may yet be victorious, but regardless of what happens, we will buy you time. Now go, all of you."

Silence fell and two knights moved to pick up the chest. Father Tourmede lead the way out of the temple and towards the cave entrance, hidden by a thick layer of brush.

Bastion and Stephen remained behind.

"Don't stray, Stephen. You will not find the cave if you lag behind."

Stephen took the man's hand in his and smiled a knowing grin of solidarity. "You have served Him well and it won't be forgotten. You are as pure as any other amongst us. You will find your way to heaven as though lead there. I bid you farewell, for we both know that you will die upon the wall."

"It is the way, Stephen. My sacrifice is but little compared to yours, for I will be delivered to heaven, as you have said, but you; you will have to content yourself with fighting the devil for the remainder of your life."

"Farewell," and the two departed company, each going about his task with great urgency, for there was no time to be wasted, Stephen catching up with the others in seconds flat for the last of them had just walked through the back door of the temple. He could see the line of men, women, and children, following Tourmede into solid brush at the foot of the mountain, an inconspicuous place indeed for a cave entrance, and he soon found himself in the cave, which surprisingly enough was lit well by crystals of unknown origin fixed in darkened veins along the walls and ceiling.

The silence in the cave was only disturbed by the steps of the single file as they made their way up the steepening climb. Lars began to fall back, others simply pushed past him with a pat on the back for comfort and encouragement. Two of the knights picked up the two youngest children, Lois and Catherine, who held tightly onto the men. Stephen could barely make out the features of those in front of him, in particular those farther up the line of advance, although the knight closest to him was quite clear with shadow and form painting the picture of a knight so bold that none could question his selflessness, the white cross of the Hospital clearly seen for what it was. He would have to get to know the men as soon as possible, to share with them his knowledge of all things surrounding the chest, as they too would have to share their inner most secrets with him, but for the time being it mattered little for they were all pure and in God's eyes floorless in both their courage and faith, just as Stephen saw it reflected by the opening of the chest: and if God could trust them, he could too.

Bastion stepped onto the wall and could see up and down the line of nine knights, each standing erect, as though on guard. Not a single one of them leant against the merlons that provided protection from the archers below. Each stood erect, waiting for the battle to commence.

The noise below them, upon the field of battle, was little at present, a few commands shouted out to soldiers of lesser rank, the cannon fodder being called to task as ladders were put together for the scaling of the defence and the building of mantlets.

"Brothers! Knights!" all turned to face Bastion as he allowed his voice to be heard. "The others have made for a hasty withdrawal, to protect the innocent, of whom you have come to know these past few months. It is for us to teach these heathen a lesson in knighthood, of what it means to be of an Order. To be a Knight of the Hospital is no easy feat; it is far easier to accept the devil into our hearts and be damned for all eternity. The service is over, the opening of the chest has been concluded. There is nothing for us now but to do our duty, to the Lord our King, to our religion, for all that we believe." He took a deep breath and looked at all once more before continuing. He drew his sword from his scabbard. "We shall not withdraw, we shall not surrender. We shall do our duty and die this day. We shall meet again in heaven." And as the last of his words were spoken an arrow pierced his head and a heinous scream filled the air. All remaining knights drew their swords and the first of the scaling ladders fell upon the battlements, the air filled with arrows, the tranquillity of the island gone forever, no longer a virgin of war but a burial place for the fallen.

The knights fought bravely, they fought as though a hundred, but the archers did their duty and with time the wall was taken. It was to the wretched Turk that the castle did fall but not a single gold coin, or anything else of any worth, could be found. For all their effort, for all those killed, the Turk departed with bitter undertones biting at their feelings of greed. Suddenly a message was received; a soldier had found a path, a way over the mountain. What purpose, other than for great necessity, could a path provide?

There was something of great value to be had on Káros, something that had so far eluded the Turks. In as quick as a wink new orders were given. A small party of men were put to station by the Galleass, the others took to banner, standard, and shield, availing themselves to the task that lay ahead.

The move up through the cave continued without rest, those of stronger virtue and ability spurring on the others. The two women, Lucia and Dorothea, began to fall well back, as did Andrew. Stephen was drawing up alongside the young lad and two women when suddenly Andrew slipped and fell, falling sideways and hitting his head against a large rock. The fall was not heard by anyone up front and the move continued, though the knight in front of Stephen quickly came to his aid.

Stephen and the knight stooped down and then knelt beside the boy, at the same time urging the others along. "Lucia, Dorothea; don't stop, keep moving. The cave goes but one way, we shall be with you shortly."

"As you wish, Stephen," came the answer from Lucia as she and her friend continued with the steep climb, trying continuously to close the widening gap. Stephen looked momentarily to his rear and saw that the last in line, a knight named Lambert, had stopped in his tracks to maintain watch on the way they had just come; Stephen then looked to the fallen.

"Andrew, Andrew, are you alright boy?" Stephen rolled the lad over and looked into his face. There was blood oozing red and thick from his head, just above the eye and slightly to the side. "Andrew, can you hear me?"

The knight placed his open palm over the boy's throat in the hope of feeling a pulse. He looked at Stephen and shook his head. "The boy is dead. He no longer breathes the air we do but has joined with Christ."

Stephen let Andrew go and stood up as did the knight. "I do not cry or feel bad for the loss."

"And why should you?" asked the knight. "I am Martin." The knight could see that Stephen was searching for an answer, even though one was not really required. "The boy's death is not of your doing. I do not know what it is to be pure. Other than what I overheard people say I do not understand why some are dead and others are still alive, but Bastion was a good friend, not just a commander-in-arms. He knew you but for the shortest time but came to know you like a brother. I know this to be true otherwise he would not have allowed us to so easily be placed under your command. I hope that we can learn of one another like brothers of the same cloth. We all hope – the other knights and I – that answers can be provided our questions, but for the time being we must be contented with the choice we have been provided. Come, Stephen, let us leave the boy here in the arms of God. We can do no more for him. We have others that must be saved and time is short."

"You are right, Martin. Our journey has just begun, and continue we must."

Both men looked upon the fallen body of Andrew one last time and departed without further word, for he was already walking alongside the lord in heaven.

"I shall tire quickly, for the climb is hard, but tell me, Stephen, was the misery of Constantinople as great as I have heard? Several of those that arrived with you were talking of the Muslim Turk and his savage ways."

"There is much savagery in war, Martin. Not all is delivered by the hand of the enemy."

"You put witness to cowardice, mercenary who cared not for the people but only their purse?" it was a statement more than a question but Stephen honoured Martin with an answer.

"The mercenary were as honourable as the citizens and the soldiers who fought for them, but there are always a few who tempt the fury of God and his allies."

"You served with such men?"

"I served beside one, not with, and he committed a heinous crime against me."

"And this crime... can you speak of it?"

Stephen stopped in his tracks and looked the knight in the eye. "He killed my wife of just two days. I buried her at sea."

Stephen turned his head to the task awaiting him and continued on his way, Martin looking on as though stunned by a horrific scene. He understood little of the emotions of man but could see that such an awful end, to a fine beginning, could easily render a man inept to show feeling against the horrors of war.

Tourmede had lead the flock to safety and as they emerged from the cave's mouth all could see the nunnery, the nuns' villa, as clear as day. The cave entrance was not sealed as the other for the approach to the island from the sea was not considered fruitful; it was also an easier path for the nuns to employ when travelling between the temple of the castle and nunnery.

Tourmede waited patiently as members of the entourage continued to file out one at a time. The first of the knights to exit was Raoul, shortly followed by Aaron and Bernard, whom between them carried the chest.

"Raoul."

"Yes, father; what is it?"

"Stand over there and watch the track. If you see anything then let me know immediately."

"Yes, father."

"Aaron, Bernard, take the chest towards the sisters' quarters," directed Tourmede of the next two knights to exit. "And tell them to gather the children and to prepare for evacuation."

"Yes, father," replied Bernard and made his way with Aaron towards the small villa of quarters, church and orphanage.

And as the others commenced to file out, one at a time, Father Tourmede asked them to step aside in order to by counted and when it came time for the final three, Stephen and the two knights, to exit, he could see that one of them was missing. "The boy, where is he."

"He fell, father," answered Stephen. "It is with regret that we left him behind, but he climb was steep and time is short."

"I won't argue with you, Stephen," and Tourmede looked amongst the gathering after giving quick prayer for Andrew. "We must go there, to the orphanage. There you are to gather together all that you need for the longest of journeys."

Stephen's eye fell upon the words and understood their meaning. "You are not coming, are you, father?"

"I must remain here. It is likely that the Turk shall require ransom, and what better ransom than a priest and his small flock—"

"You shall be killed and the sisters will be raped," Stephen finished for him.

Tourmede had the most pleasant and unselfish look upon his face that moment and spoke softly for all to hear. "We don't know that, Stephen. Besides, there is no room upon the carrack. I shall take the sisters into hiding here on the island; the Turks will not find us, with any luck. They are here out of greed and cannot support themselves for long. They will depart soon enough. But you; you must make haste with the children, take the knights for protection... all five know how to sail, each came from Lepanto before being stationed here in Káros, and have each made many

170

voyages across the Mediterranean and the Aegean." He directed those that stood in wait, ordering them to continue. "Stay with the knights and the chest, help the nuns prepare the children." And as the small group commenced to follow the chest bearers Aaron and Bernard, Tourmede made final insistence. "And you, Stephen, remain with me," and then with silent indication he requested that Lambert and Martin should go and stand with Raoul.

When alone Stephen prompted Tourmede to say what it was that he wished to say. "We are alone, father. What is it you wish of me?"

"No more than God would ask." Tourmede looked about and found a couple of small boulders. "Please, let us sit for a few minutes and discuss something of importance."

"Do we have time?"

"We have to make time, Stephen, for if you were to depart now then your task will never be met."

"You have me intrigued."

"That is good, now sit." Tourmede allowed himself a few seconds of private thought before continuing as best he could.

"With the time I had alone with the chest and Father Norotus, much was discussed. I revealed to him some ancient texts that I had in my library—," a holler suddenly broke his concentration.

"Father," yelled Lambert. "I see movement. We have but limited time; one half of the sands in an upturned glass is all you have."

"Maintain your position!" and to Stephen he continued. "We have time, now listen to me and listen carefully. The scripture on the chest, beneath, upon its sides and that on top, all is written in the Semitic language of Jesus, Aramaic, it is a codex from the secret gospel of Christ, Himself. Only one such copy of the gospel exists... to my knowledge," Tourmede grasp Stephen by the hands to silence him for he was about to speak. "We have no time, listen and listen alone. I did not see into the chest but I know what it contains. Norotus knows, but he has passed from this world, and although he has proven to be impure, he still walks in heaven. It is Jesus, his saviour, who died for our sins, He will protect him

171

against the voice of God, His father, for the Old Testament is not as forgiving as the New.

"The codex is clear to me and I shall reveal it to you, but if you should require further information then you must travel to the port of Southern France, and only there shall the truth be revealed. You seek Father Ambaedian. He can show you more if required and he is as pure as them all.

"Now listen to me with all your heart. One of the passages upon the chest reads: "He shall know his way, upon his quest, travelling far, as bequest, to surrender life, so dear and strong, his way will be painted, with voices strung", And beneath the chest; "only the purest of mind and body will survive the contents of the chest". A test, Stephen, it is but a test. I don't know how it came about but the chest contains several items of sacred importance.

"Listen to me, Stephen. The items are good and bad, the same as the Old and the New, Testaments that preach from different perspective. The items must be joined in order for the power of the contents to be held at bay. You, Stephen, you are the one that can survive the contents of the chest; I know this, I feel it."

"I cannot—"

"A voice came to me, Stephen. You must trust in the Lord's decision."

Stephen knew that time was short and continued to listen with unblemished attention.

"I don't understand everything, nor do I claim it, but it seems to me that it is but a test, that God and the devil are one, a test that must be passed in order to prove oneself, and Jesus is but the son of God. You can only commit crime against the commandments by committing such heinous and unforgivable acts against the pure. Those who have attained the true belief of God, of the scripture, will survive the contents of the chest, but fused together, joining the good with the bad, that will reveal to the world the meaning of life, and that is to 'deny the devil'.

"A Muslim cannot be affected, for his belief belongs to Allah: he has already been recruited by the devil and his false worship. It is for them that they have failed the test of honour, faith and all

172

values associated with good, clean, moralistic servitude. Fuse the good and the bad, Stephen. This is the first of your many quests."

"Fuse them?"

"It is written, so it must be done," said Tourmede. "Listen to me. Jesus came to the world and delivered himself to the cross for all of us to be forgiven our sins, now, in all His glory, he delivers to us again, His power, for he is allowing us, mortal man, to be free of impurity. Fuse the good and the bad, and all will be glorious in His name."

"Father, it is time. They come running, no more sand is left. If we do not leave now we shall fall into the hands of the enemy," said Lambert with the greatest of concern.

Father Tourmede stood. "Then let us depart. Come, let us go."

There was much activity being undertaken by the time Tourmede and Stephen had arrived to the front of the nuns' villa, their quarters and small out-of-the-way church having been turned into an orphanage. The children had been gathered to the front of the building and seemed to be in good order; all were quiet and each carried a small parcel of extra clothing.

Stephen could see the sisters moving around in a state of calmness, keeping the children from being frightened, and Lois and Catherine were there too, helping their soon-to-be newfound-friends with preparing for the short walk to the sea, where the carrack waited for its precious cargo.

Aaron and Bernard were already halfway down the track, heading towards the hidden harbour that consisted of little more than a few planks of wood made fast to a few posts between solid mountains of rock. Lars was up the front, looking left and right as he made his descent from the side of the mountain and down the track to their escape.

Father Tourmede introduced one of the sisters. "Stephen, this is Sister Anne."

"I am pleased to meet you, Stephen," she bowed slightly.

"The honour is mine, sister."

"I hear you are to look after the children, taking them to a safe haven."

"I shall do all that I can."

"I am sure that you will," and Anne looked to the others, namely Lois and Catherine. "I see you have already had your hands troubled by the torments of young minds."

"They are a pleasure, as it is my pleasure to serve."

"I wish I had time to get to know you, Stephen. I am sure that Father Tourmede will advise me accordingly once we have taken to hiding."

"I hope he will be kind," said Stephen as he turned to see the children commence their short trek, the knights Raoul and Lambert having returned from their watch on the track to lead them away; and Martin arrived at his side.

"Excuse me, father, sister, but it is time for us to go. The enemy will be here shortly."

"Thank you, Martin," said Tourmede who put his hand out to shake that of the knights. "It has been a pleasure serving with you. Tell the others, when you get the chance, that the key and the chest must be protected at all costs, except that of the innocent," and without the meaning of his glance being seen by Sister Anne, Tourmede looked out the corner of his eye and towards the children, meaning that their lives were more important than the chest and their sacred religion.

"All of my time here has been spent listening to the grand view in thinking that the chest was all important," said Martin. "But I see now why you are pure of heart and soul, for you would give up all that you believe in to protect those of little understanding."

"Goodbye, Martin, and goodbye to you, Stephen, Templar Knight of Constantinople, Esteemed Friend of Constantine, and Saviour of Christ's Belongings."

"Goodbye, father."

174

"Oh, Stephen, one last thing," and he reached into his pocket and pulled out the key, handing it the Templar without further word.

A few smiles were all that time permitted for and to their separate ways they did depart. Stephen looked over his shoulder as he made his way towards the carrack and saw for himself, Father Tourmede and the sisters of Káros heading for sanctuary upon the island of rock they had known for so long, priest and nuns, of Orthodox and Latin, running as best their legs could carry them, away from the Turkish advance. One more surprise was then met, for as he turned to press on with his coming engagement he could see Lucia and Dorothea, waving to him with a smile, before they too turned tail, and ran after the sisters and Father Tourmede: they had just then sacrificed themselves for the sake of the children and the chest.

The carrack was boarded with little fuss, apart from the fact that the eleven children, new to the vestiges provided by a vessel of the seven seas, were upset. The children had been to sea before, sure enough, but the horrors of those days, where torment upon torment was suffered, handed out by the hand of those of Muslim faith, to be surrendered to a harem of insignificant importance; it all managed to shroud the experience.

The knights went about their work and set the sails, the carrack moving with a groan, manoeuvred slowly towards the open sea.

Lars contented himself with aiding the children, showing a smile and plenty of affection, Lois and Catherine acting as though adults, having experienced enough themselves to know better, mature of mind and action, as pure as any other that had confronted the opening of the chest.

Stephen looked out upon the island as they moved further and further away, the sun slowly sinking in the horizon, similar to the way it did when he was making his escape from Constantinople, having buried his wife at sea. This, for him, was a cruel moment, where the memories of Clover came flooding back. Of all the things he did and did not know, one thing was for sure; he would never again lay eyes upon Káros.

"Abu, Abu," shouted the sailor as he scrambled into the captain's quarters.

Abu turned slowly, disgust showing on his face, for very little impressed him of the men that served beneath him.

"What is it, Ibrahim?"

"A boat, Abu, it looks like a carrack. The alert has come from the lookout."

"How far, Ibrahim? How many hours, how many days?" for he despised the worthless crew that he commanded.

"Within a day, if that is your wish, Abu."

"No! No, no, no; that won't do." He thought for a second. "A carrack you say?"

"Yes Abu."

"We shall head for the island, Ibrahim, and see if we can't find ourselves the brigantine. Then, and only then, shall I allow myself to make a decision. It is possible that our quarry have purchased themselves a new vessel, in which case we shall follow from behind, hidden by the waves and the horizon." Abu held his open palm up to prevent further words and interruption; he was thinking. "Order for the watch to be maintained. If my assumption is correct we will be following that carrack within a day, to follow it like a fox follows its prey, and when the time is right we shall pounce."

Ibrahim smiled, and a little chuckle escaped him. "Ah, Abu, so grand it is to work beneath you; so grand it is indeed."